"I'm happy with my life the way it is," Harri said lightly.

"Even if you can't get a man to look at you?" Shae teased, lying back in the grass, his eyes closed.

"Maybe you're tired of living, huh, Shae?" Sitting up, she reached for her cup, empty now except for some melting ice. Tipping the cup forward, she let a stream of icy water trickle down the front of his shirt.

Without opening his eyes, his hands reached out to capture hers. "Women have died for less than that," he said calmly.

She laughed, trying to free herself from his hold. Rolling to his side, he pinned her to the ground. They struggled, rolling around on the blanket as she pitted her strength against his. She was overpowered and knew it. "Shae, stop it! We're attracting attention," she warned breathlessly.

He held her firmly in place and retrieved an ice cube, then shoved it down the front of her dress. He laughed when she protested indignantly. "What's the matter, Harriet, can't take your own medicine?"

"Shae!"

"Okay, I'll take it out." He reached for it but her hand blocked his.

"Hold it."

He smiled, and she felt her breath catch. "I remember a time you wouldn't have stopped me. . . ."

WHAT ARE *LOVESWEPT* ROMANCES?

They are stories of true romance and touching emotion. We believe those two very important ingredients are constants in our highly sensual and very believable stories in the *LOVESWEPT* line. Our goal is to give you, the reader, stories of consistently high quality that may sometimes make you laugh, sometimes make you cry, but are always fresh and creative and contain many delightful surprises within their pages.

Most romance fans read an enormous number of books. Those they truly love, they keep. Others may be traded with friends and soon forgotten. We hope that each *LOVESWEPT* romance will be a treasure—a "keeper." We will always try to publish

LOVE STORIES YOU'LL NEVER FORGET
BY AUTHORS YOU'LL ALWAYS REMEMBER

The Editors

LOVESWEPT® • 387

Lori Copeland
Darling Deceiver

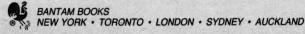
BANTAM BOOKS
NEW YORK • TORONTO • LONDON • SYDNEY • AUCKLAND

DARLING DECEIVER

A Bantam Book / March 1990

LOVESWEPT® and the wave device are registered
trademarks of Bantam Books, a division of
Bantam Doubleday Dell Publishing Group, Inc.
Registered in U.S. Patent
and Trademark Office and elsewhere.

If you would be interested in receiving protective vinyl
covers for your Loveswept books, please write to this address
for information:

Loveswept
Bantam Books
P.O. Box 985
Hicksville, NY 11802

ISBN 0-553-44020-9

Published simultaneously in the United States and Canada

Bantam Books are published by Bantam Books, a division
of Bantam Doubleday Dell Publishing Group, Inc. Its trademark, consisting of the words "Bantam Books" and the
portrayal of a rooster, is Registered in U.S. Patent and
Trademark Office and in other countries. Marca Registrada.
Bantam Books, 666 Fifth Avenue, New York, New York 10103.

PRINTED IN THE UNITED STATES OF AMERICA

OPM   0   9   8   7   6   5   4   3   2   1

One

"Miserable piece of junk!"

Shae jammed the stubborn screen back into the door frame, then paused to catch his breath. How did he get into these messes, he wondered.

Glancing up, he squinted against the hot sun, still a blistering red ball on the western horizon. To the north, a dark cloud bank offered the only hope of relief from the sweltering heat that he'd seen in days.

His arm came up to wipe the sweat trickling down the side of his face. There should be a law against this kind of humidity!

Leaning back on the ladder, Shae studied the warped screen door in disgust. This old house was turning out to be nothing but a headache. When Gram had willed the house to Shae's father Jess, she'd thought she was doing him a favor—and she might have been if Jess had sold it as Shae had suggested. But Shae's father rarely did as he was told.

Jess Malone was one hell of a literary agent, but in his role as a wise and knowing father, the jury was still out.

Shae recalled how Jess had persuaded him to come back to Cloverdale. Father and son had sat up half the night in a little bar in midtown Manhattan, eating pretzels and drinking beer while Jess had convinced Shae that it was the only sensible thing to do.

Shae, you need to buckle down, son. Spend the summer in Cloverdale. There isn't a thing in that sleepy little burg to distract you from your work. Close the apartment, move to the suburbs, and concentrate on the book.

"And I listened to him again," Shae muttered.

You'll be a lot more productive, son. You'll have the book done in nothing flat.

Productive? Shae would be lucky if he didn't die of boredom before the summer was over. As soon as he finished repairing this screen, he was going to lock himself in the office and not come out until he'd finished his book.

Once it was polished, he'd burn blue smoke getting back to New York and civilization.

He studied the warped screen door again. Cloverdale. Bah! Why had he given in to Jess? He knew all about Cloverdale. Hadn't he spent every summer here as a boy—even lived with Gram for a couple of years in his early teens?

He'd loved Elinore Malone, but he'd always been glad to see summer come to an end. Nothing went on in Cloverdale except the street lights, at exactly seven o'clock every evening.

For absolutely no reason at all, the year he spent

attending the local school and the image of Harriet Whitlock popped into his mind. His mouth suddenly went dry, and sweat began to trickle down the sides of his face.

What in the world had made him think of *her?*

Harriet—the name still had the power to make him break out in a cold sweat. She had made his life a living hell back in junior high.

She had stalked him though the halls as if he were a hunted animal, humiliating him in front of his friends, idolizing him with her eyes, tormenting him with her idiotic letters and poems which declared her everlasting, burning love.

And the day she had stood up in the lunchroom and proclaimed to the entire third hour lunch period that *fate* had destined her to be his chosen one, Shae had wanted to crawl into a hole.

A shudder started at the base of his spine and shot straight up to his shoulder blades whenever he recalled that black day in his life. It had taken months for him to live it down.

Since Harriet had lived next door to Gram, there had been no way for him to escape her. She'd always been there, draped in front of her bedroom window on the second story, her arms propped on the window sill, her eyes openly adoring him.

Harriet the Curse. The weirdest girl in seventh grade—and she'd had to pick him to be her "chosen" one.

He could almost laugh about it now, but back when he'd been in the throes of puberty, the thought of Harriet hadn't been so amusing.

Damn, was he glad he'd seen the last of her.

Studying the warped screen again, he grappled

with his conscience. Should he just close this house and go back to his maintenance-free apartment in Manhattan? If he was going to be spending all his time making repairs to the dilapidated house, he wouldn't get any work done.

He had just reached up to wipe the sweat from his eyes when his forearm suddenly froze in mid-air.

Coming—no, *slithering*—across the patio was a snake—not just any snake, a big snake.

As he eased a step up the ladder, his eyes widened as it moved across the patio, heading straight for the open doorway.

Realizing where the snake was headed, Shae's hand shot out to close the screen door. But the warped frame still refused to budge.

His eyes glued to the large reptile, Shae grasped the frame and jiggled it. The screen door didn't budge, so he hopped to the top rung of the ladder and using both hands, he rattled the frame frantically.

This snake wasn't a small, harmless garden variety; it was a big, thick, "get out of my way—I'm coming through" kind of snake.

A python, Shae realized. The damn thing was a python!

Stunned, he scrambled to the top of the ladder and jerked his feet up to his chest as he felt the reptile's thick body bump against the side of the ladder, then ooze through the open doorway.

It took a few moments for Shae to realize that the snake had actually entered his house.

When reality finally sank in, he gradually lowered his feet a few rungs and bent down, trying to peer around the drapes into the house.

There was no sign of the snake anywhere.

Slumping against the ladder, he tried to think. What should he do now?

His eyes traveled helplessly back to the open doorway. Should he call for help?

In the distance he could hear the sound of a power mower. The smell of freshly cut grass mingled pleasantly with the aroma of pork chops frying in a skillet.

A dog barked nearby, and he could hear the faint sounds of children's laughter as they splashed in a nearby backyard pool.

He realized that it had been years since he had returned to Cloverdale. The neighborhood had changed. It seemed that younger families were living here now, and Shae wasn't familiar with any of them.

His gaze returned to the doorway as he began to ease his way back down the ladder.

No, he couldn't ask a neighbor for help. No one in his right mind would go into a house with a snake that size.

Moving to the doorway, he peered inside the living room's dark interior.

Nothing.

Even though the sun was still blazing, he reached through the doorway to flip on the light switch. His eyes searched around the room guardedly.

Still no sign of the snake.

Where had the thing gone?

Taking a deep breath, Shae stepped inside the house. He wasn't a coward. He could handle an ordinary snake.

But this snake isn't ordinary, Malone. It's BIG.

His gaze darted around the combined dining and family room as he cautiously edged his way toward the kitchen.

Once there, he fumbled in the drawer next to the refrigerator for the telephone book.

Grasping the directory, he withdrew it and tucked it under his arm. As he backed cautiously out of the room, he grabbed the desk phone, thanking his lucky stars that it was attached to an extra long cord. He picked his way carefully as he moved back to the security of the patio.

Thumbing hurriedly through the pages, he located the number of the police department.

The phone was answered on the second ring.

"Cloverdale Police. Sergeant Coffman."

"Yeah, listen . . . I've got a problem over here."

"What kind of a problem?"

"A snake just crawled inside my house."

"Yeah?"

"A big snake."

"How big?"

"Big enough to scare the hell out of me," Shae said.

There was a meaningful pause, then, "How big?"

"Big," Shae said again, glancing nervously back to the open doorway. "Look, my name's Shae Malone. I live at 6428 Sheridan Drive, and I want a squad car—no, two squad cars—over here on the double!"

"Now, just calm down, Mr. Malone. You want to give me that address again?" The officer's voice remained polite, but unimpressed.

Shae seethed. He was sure the man would act quickly if he were the one with a python roaming through his hallways. "6428 Sheridan Drive," Shae repeated.

"6428 Sheridan Drive. How big did you say this snake is?"

"I don't know . . . six to seven feet long and maybe eight or nine inches thick."

There was another significant pause on the other end of the line, then a monotone voice repeated, "Six to seven feet long and eight or nine inches thick."

"Yes."

"You're sure?"

Sweat trickled down the sides of Shae's face. "No, I was bored, officer, so I thought, hey, what the hell, Malone, why don't you call the police and make up this big story about this snake crawling into your hou—of course I'm sure! The thing looks like a python to me!"

"A python?"

"That's right, a p-y-t-h-o-n. A B-I-G p-y-t-h-o-n." He spelled it out this time.

"Then maybe we'd better contact the people at the zoo."

"Contact whomever you want," Shae said tersely, "just get the thing out of my house."

"Right away, Mr. Malone—oh, and as a precaution, close all the outside doors so he can't get out," the officer suggested.

"Don't kid yourself. If that snake wants to leave, I won't stop him."

The officer chuckled. "Hold tight, Mr. Malone. We'll have a car over there in ten minutes."

Shae snapped the receiver back into its cradle, then moved another rung up the ladder.

He had a feeling this was going to be the longest ten minutes of his life.

•   •   •

Harri walked into the living room, and Myron gave her a wolf whistle, followed by an enthusiastic, "What a bod!"

"Thank you, Myron, from the bottom of my heart," she said.

Myron decided to pile it on. "Great legs, too!"

"And personality and charm," Harri added. Myron was turning out to be quite a charmer, even if the Asian mynah bird was half blind.

She was still smiling as she reached for her copy of the New York Times best-selling murder mystery *Murder, She Cried.*

The book had gone on sale in paperback today, and she couldn't wait to read it. Perry Beal was the best: the man was a genius.

Caring for a menagerie had at least given her some free time at home, she reasoned as she positioned the bowl of popcorn next to her father's chintz-covered chair.

When fire had broken out in the zoo's infirmary last month, Mike had panicked. That afternoon, he'd called a meeting in his office of all personnel to discuss what to do with the animals until renovation could be completed.

Since the animals required a controlled environment, the problem was a sticky one. No one wanted to take a monkey, a lion cub, a mynah bird, or any of the other animals home.

But before Harri had realized what was happening, Mike had appointed *her* as the animals' temporary guardian. She wasn't thrilled by the assignment, but since she was softhearted she had agreed.

Harri glanced at the lion cub stretched out on her mother's Persian rug. Of course, her mom wasn't going to be exactly ecstatic about having a menagerie living in her house, that was if Harri ever got around to telling her about the unorthodox arrangement.

Switching on the lamp beside the chair, Harri heard the first low rumble of thunder. Tingling with anticipation, she dropped into the chair and got comfortable. A thunderstorm. This was going to be a perfect night to lose herself in a world of high finance, sex, and intrigue.

And no one could create that better than Perry Beal.

After opening the book, Harri read the first page out loud to Myron . . .

Something was wrong. The premonition had been with Anne all day, and yet logic told her that she had no reason to be afraid. There was nothing in her grandmother's house to frighten her . . . was there?

Drawing a shaky breath, Anne started to climb the familiar winding stairway leading to her room, the room she'd grown up in, always felt so secure in—so protected. Her fears were groundless. Once she was in the old feather bed, watching the shadows outside her window dancing on the wall, she would feel better. Of course . . . there was absolutely nothing wrong. She was just tired, that was all.

Then she heard it—

The phone jangled beside her chair, and Harri nearly jumped out of her skin.

Groaning aloud, she wished she had remembered to switch on the answering machine.

Magnolia bolted from the bedroom, the television

remote control still gripped firmly in her paw. The spider monkey had been engrossed in watching *The Newlywed Game* when the phone had shattered her concentration.

Harri reluctantly picked up the receiver. "Yes?"

"Ms. Whitlock?"

"Yes?"

"This is Sergeant Coffman with the Cloverdale Police Department."

She frowned. "Yes?"

"Would you happen to be missing a python, ma'am?"

"A python—" Harri sat up straighter. "Florence!"

"Well, I don't believe the snake stopped for introductions, but we have a report from a man living at 6428 Sheridan Drive who says a very large snake has just crawled into his house."

"Oh, dear." Harri realized immediately that Magnolia must have been tampering with the latch on Florence's cage again. "I'm sorry, officer. What was that address again?"

"6428."

Elinore's house. "I'm sorry, officer. I'll go after Florence, immediately."

"Thank you, ma'am. I have a couple of officers on their way to assist you."

Harri put the phone back in the cradle, sending Magnolia a reproachful look. "Did you let Florence out of her cage?"

The monkey chattered nervously, then turned and fled back to the safety of the bedroom.

Harri sighed. "You did."

Reaching for a napkin to mark her place in the book, she left the character Anne in a very precarious position.

Chances were Anne would manage, but then with Perry Beal you could never really be sure.

Sighing again, Harri closed the book and went to rescue her new neighbor.

Two

Elinore Malone had passed away two years earlier, leaving her charming Victorian house on Sheridan Drive vacant. It was rumored that Elinore had left the house to her son, but since no one had moved in, Harri did not know for certain. One thing Harri did know: for the past couple of nights she had seen a light burning in one of the bedroom windows.

She hadn't met her new neighbor, and under these circumstances she couldn't say that she was looking forward to it. Florence had probably scared the poor soul half out of his or her wits, she thought as she stood on the porch and pressed the doorbell. Though Florence wouldn't hurt a fly, Harri knew from experience some people were hard to reassure.

Still, she had to admit that having a python show up on your doorstep would put a blight on anyone's day.

Failing to receive a response at the front door, Harri started around to the back of the house. The old house showed visible signs of neglect: weeds were peeking through the bricks on the patio, the shrubs were badly in need of a trim, and the swimming pool needed a thorough scrubbing.

Elinore's house had been a showplace when she'd been alive, and Harri thought it was inexcusable for her heirs to let the house run down this way.

But then Elinore had probably left her house to her son, Jess, and if Jess was anything like his son, Shae, the neglect was understandable.

Shae Malone.

Harri realized she hadn't thought about him in years. The name brought to mind her teenage years, and she quickly dismissed the painful memories. Thank heaven those years were behind her. As a teenager she had really made a fool of herself over him.

Coming around the corner of the house, her footsteps slowed as she spotted a man perched on the top rung of a ladder.

Her pulse quickened, and she suddenly found it difficult to breathe. Staring at the stranger, she prayed that her eyes were deceiving her. It couldn't be . . . her imagination was playing tricks on her again. Just because for the first time in years she'd happened to think of Shae Malone, that couldn't be him sitting on that ladder.

But her vision was still a perfect twenty-twenty, she realized a few moments later. It was clear that fate had thrown her another curve.

The man balanced on top of the ladder was Shae Malone.

Good-looking, cocksure, arrogant Shae Malone.

Harri felt her pulse begin to beat faster. The years

had been kind to Shae—too kind. Most of the boys with whom she'd attended Cloverdale Junior High were already cursed with receding hairlines, expanding waistlines, and bifocals, but not Shae.

If anything, he was even handsomer than she'd remembered: his eyes seemed a more startling shade of blue, his hair a darker, more striking shade of red.

It wasn't fair, she thought resentfully. He'd *always* been Mr. Perfect. She could only hope that when she took a closer look he would show signs of developing a paunch.

She forced herself to step closer, aware that he wasn't going to be thrilled to see her again. And she couldn't say that she blamed him. She'd had a terrible crush on him during the years that they were growing up.

She had pursued him relentlessly, shamelessly. Her cheeks flooded with color even now, fifteen years later, at the memory of how she had thrown herself at his feet and practically begged for him to notice her.

But he hadn't returned her adoration. He'd ignored her. Simply ignored her.

If she had a penny for every time he'd told her to get lost, she could vacation in Paris for a year.

She'd been madly infatuated with him, and she had to admit she had done her share to provoke him at times. There was the incident when she'd chained his bicycle to his grandmother's front porch so that he couldn't go bike riding with Sally Collier one fourth of July . . . hoping he'd stay home with her. And the time she'd painted his name on his baseball bat upset him, but that had been an honest mistake. She'd thought he would have been proud of her handiwork. He was the only boy in the neighborhood who had a ballbat with his name on it.

Harri squared her shoulders, and her footsteps picked up tempo. But all that nonsense had taken place when they were both adolescents. They were adults now, capable of laughing about those years now. But it sure hadn't been funny then.

And she would remind him of that if he started to dart for cover, the way he always had the moment he'd seen her coming. *Right, Harri. It's the first time you've seen the guy in fifteen years, and your python has just crawled into his house.*

Great start, Harriet. He's going to really be impressed by your "maturity."

"Shae Malone."

He turned in the direction of her voice, and his features flushed and then turned a sickly white.

It wasn't hard for Harri to read his expression, even from this distance. It was an unmistakable "Oh, hell! it's her again." And she resented it.

"Harriet? Harriet Whitlock!" His voice cracked. *Cracked!*

She smothered the urge to blurt out a resentful "Yes, so what?" back at him, but with admirable restraint she settled for a nice smile, and a pleasantly modulated, "Hello, Shae. It's been a long time."

Oh, he looked good all right. Too darned good. She forced her eyes to focus on anything but the broad expanse of his chest. He was wearing a neatly trimmed beard now, a devastating addition since the last time she'd seen him—but then he'd only been fifteen when she'd last seen him, and how many fifteen-year-olds grew a beard?

Wearing white shorts, a navy blue shirt, and white running shoes, she could see a maturity in him now, a hardness that made him even more virile, more attractive, more hopelessly inaccessible than ever.

And she couldn't find the slightest hint of a beer belly. Just flat, taut muscle stretched across a slim, enviable waist.

"What are *you* doing here?" he asked.

"*I'm* with the zoo," she returned sharply—a little too sharply, and caught herself. "I'm with the zoo," she repeated.

"The zoo—? That's *your* snake in there?"

Shae was stunned. *Good Lord! Harriet Whitlock?* It was hard to believe that the slender, blond-haired, amber-eyed beauty walking toward him was *Harriet Whitlock.* What had happened to the scrawny little kid with the strange-colored eyes, the crazy pig tails, and weird clothes?

"I'm sorry if Florence scared you." Keep calm, she told herself. Watch your posture, Harri. If she stood up straight, acted like a perfect lady, maybe she wouldn't make a fool of herself.

Harri paused at the foot of the ladder to look up at him. Her pulse quickened, and her stomach felt as if someone had just slammed into it with a steel fist as he stared down at her.

"You're really Harriet?" he asked again.

"Yes, I'm really Harriet." He was not going to rattle her. She would get the snake, then get the devil out of here. "Where's Florence?"

"Florence?"

Harri stared back a him evenly. "The snake?"

"You still live next door?"

She could see he was having a hard time associating her with the Harriet of days gone by, and she liked that. She didn't consider herself to be a raving beauty, but then she wasn't so bad. He'd been a fool to treat her so shabbily, and she just hoped he could finally see that.

"No, I live on the other side of town. I'm housesitting for my parents while they're off on an extended sabbatical in Europe."

"And you're keeping a snake in their house?"

"Just until the new building is completed." She felt herself growing defensive again. "There was a fire at the zoo's infirmary two weeks ago."

Shae felt his skin crawl. "The damn thing doesn't get out often, does it?"

"No . . . rarely."

Shae began to ease down the ladder. "Rarely? Why does that fail to console me?"

Harri stepped back and waited until Shae's feet touched ground. He had a nice athletic body, the kind splashed across billboards or book jackets.

Nervously brushing her palms down the sides of her jeans, she added, "I really am sorry about this, but Florence is perfectly harmless."

Shae mumbled something under his breath, and unless she missed her guess, it was an unflattering remark about her ability to perform her job.

"I had no idea you were back in Cloverdale," she said.

"I'm only here for the summer."

"Elinore left her house to you?"

"To Dad, actually, but I'm trying to convince him to put it up for sale this fall."

"Oh." Harri was annoyed the instant she felt the

familiar prick of disappointment. Why should she care what he did? The sooner the house sold, the better. Maybe someone would move in who would take better care of it.

"Do you have any idea where Florence is now?" Harri fell into step behind Shae as they started toward the open doorway.

"She didn't mention her itinerary," he said.

"I know what you must be thinking, but I can assure you this has never happened before." She had to hurry to keep up with his long strides.

They glanced up as two officers came walking around the corner of the house carrying notepads.

"Is this the party who reported a snake in his house?" one asked.

"Yes." Shae nodded toward the open doorway. "In there."

The officers glanced at one another warily. "It says here the snake is a python?"

Shae nodded. "That's what it looked like to me."

Noting the look the officers shot one another, Harri stepped forward. "Gentlemen, I'm responsible for the snake, and I'll see that it's removed right away."

The two officers looked so thankful that Harri grinned.

"We'd be real grateful, ma'am."

Glancing back at Shae, Harri said quietly, "Florence likes cool, dark places. I'd guess she's either in one of your closets or the bathroom."

Shae paled beneath his tan, "Okay . . . so?"

"If you'll just point the way."

"We'll be close by if you need any help," one of the officers offered.

Sure you will, Harri thought. Close by your car, ready to run.

Stepping cautiously into the house's interior, Shae paused, listening to the soft hum of the air conditioner.

"The main bath is down this hall," he whispered.

"That's probably where she is," Harri whispered back, wondering why they were whispering at all.

She took the lead, and Shae followed a safe distance behind. Making their way down the dim hallway, they peered into each vacant room.

When Harri suddenly stopped and brought her hand up to her nose to block a sneeze, Shae nearly fainted.

Glancing back at him, she apologized. "Sorry, my allergies have been acting up."

Sagging against the wall, he took a deep breath to steady himself. Sweat was visible on his forehead now. "Doesn't this make you nervous?" he whispered hoarsely.

"No, I've handled snakes for years." Harri glanced at the large boxes strewn around the room, allowing Shae sufficient time to swallow his heart that had just lodged in his throat. "I see you're still unpacking."

"Yes, but I'm not getting anywhere. I'll be living out of boxes for the next few months." Fumbling in his back pocket, he drew out a large handkerchief as a clap of thunder shook the house.

"Sounds like rain," she said. "We could use some."

"Have summers gotten hotter here?"

She ignored his question. "What brings you back to Cloverdale?" she asked with deliberately calculated indifference. She would not let him see that she still found him incredibly attractive.

Shae finished mopping his brow and stuck the

handkerchief back in his pocket. "I'm was hoping for a little peace and quiet."

The irony in his tone was unmistakable.

"Well, you've came to the right place. You know Cloverdale, dull as dishwater."

They began to move down the hallway again.

The second room on the right revealed stacks of boxes filled with books, but no Florence.

The contents of the next room were the same. A computer was resting on a table that had been shoved carelessly against the wall. Stacks of papers and books, and a lone coffee cup testified that they had all been used recently.

But still no snake.

Harri paused at the doorway, looking around the small office. "Do you work at home?"

Shae nodded distractedly. "I'm trying to finish—" He caught himself, glanced at her uneasily, and broke off in mid-sentence.

Her brow lifted. "You're trying to finish?"

The strangest look came over his face. "A book," he murmured.

She stared back at him expectantly. "A what?"

"A book," he repeated.

"A book?"

"Yes . . . a book."

"You write books?"

He shrugged. "I try."

"Oh . . . are you published?"

It was on the tip of his tongue to confess that he was, that his first book had zoomed to the top of the lists, and that he had produced nothing but best-sellers since.

He started to tell her that he was Perry Beal, but

something about the way she was looking at him made him stop.

All of a sudden Harriet Whitlock materialized, staring at him with those big, strange golden brown eyes. . . . If she ever found out that he was a published writer, she would drive him nuts again! No matter *how* attractive he found the adult Harriet, his memories of the youthful version lingered. He wasn't sure if her sophistication extended to her personality.

He shrugged lamely, and she understood the gesture to mean that he wasn't published.

"Thanks to Gram, I have enough money to live on this summer while I finish the book," he hedged, hoping she'd buy the vague excuse.

"Oh . . . you're living on your inheritance?" *Poor guy, using up all his money in search of a fantasy,* she thought. An apologetic smile appeared at the corners of her mouth. "I'm sorry." Her eyes returned to the computer again. "Well, it looks like you're trying hard enough."

Shae's gaze carefully avoided meeting hers. "Yes, I work at it."

He felt guilty for the deception, but knowing the old Harriet, he decided to take things slowly. He wasn't a masochist.

"What are you trying to write?"

Shae shrugged. "Mystery."

She sighed. "I love to read mysteries—Perry Beal's my favorite author. Have you ever read any of his books?"

"One or two."

"He's good, isn't he?"

"He's a little wordy."

They moved on, pausing at the entrance to the bathroom.

Harri stepped inside and flipped on the light. She pushed the shower curtain aside, and Shae heard her sigh with relief as she found Florence curled contentedly around the shower head.

"There you are! Shame on you!"

Shae flattened himself against the wall, his face paling to an ashen gray as he eyed the snake. Goosebumps sprang up on his arms, and he pressed against the wall more tightly. "She's big," he said weakly.

"Not really." Harri leaned across the tub and ran her hands over the snake affectionately. "Florence is actually small for her age. That's why she's in the zoo's infirmary. I'm trying to get her fattened up a little." Glancing at him, she grinned at the way Shae had almost blended into the pattern on the wallpaper. "If Florence were a normal size, I wouldn't be able to handle her alone."

As her voice faded, Shae's gaze suddenly focused on her shapely bottom. Damn, she had changed! Her jeans fit her like a glove, nipping in at her narrow waist and conforming to an unbelievable pair of legs. This couldn't be Harriet Whitlock. She was pulling his leg.

"Come on, Florence, it's time to go back to your cage." Harri's voice came back to him as her head emerged from the tub. She glanced at him apologetically. "I hate to ask, but do you think you could help me?"

Shae's heart sprang to his throat. "To do what?"

"If you could just grab Florence, and slide her into my arms?"

Shae swallowed, trying to keep his head. "Do I have a choice?"

"Not if you want Florence out of your tub tonight."

"I want Florence out of my life permanently."

Easing forward, he made himself think about Ms. January on the calendar hanging in his office. He was certain that if he thought about what he was actually doing, he would be sick.

"That's it, just lift her a little—yes, that's great."

Ms. January—great legs, sultry, pouty mouth, terrific—

Cringing, he lifted the python and let it slide into Harri's arms. Hurriedly he jumped back to safety.

"Are you sure you can handle that thing?" Shae thought Harri looked too small to be lugging around anything that size, although he didn't know what he would do if she couldn't handle the snake.

He sure wasn't going to carry it for her.

Harri started down the hall with Shae following at a wholesome distance. When they reached the open patio door, she turned to face him. "Well, sorry about the inconvenience. It's been nice to see you again."

As she said goodbye, she fleetingly wondered if he was married. The disturbing possibility hadn't occurred to her before now. "If you . . . or your wife need anything—flour, sugar, coffee—you're welcome to borrow from me," she said.

She would keep calm. She wouldn't overdo it. She should be polite, then leave while she was still ahead.

Shae paused in the hallway, determined to keep a healthy distance between himself and the snake.

He smiled. "Thanks, I'm not married, but you and your husband feel free to do the same."

"I'm not married. I lost my husband two years ago."

Who in his right mind had married Harriet Whitlock? he wondered.

"I'm sorry—did you marry someone local?"

"Yes, Patrick Mulligan."

"Irish? You married Irish?" he exclaimed.

Patrick Mulligan had been Cloverdale's star athlete. He'd gone on to play college football, and Shae remembered Gram mentioning in one of her last letters that he'd signed to play with the Denver Broncos.

Harri's features tightened as she recognized Shae's startled expression. "Yes, Patrick and I were married—and don't look so stunned."

"I didn't mean it that way. I'm just shocked to hear about Patrick . . . I'm sorry."

Harriet had actually snagged Patrick Mulligan? The best catch in Cloverdale? Shae found that incredible.

"Well, take care." Harri stepped onto the patio, then turned to call over her shoulder, "And don't worry, you'll have nothing but peace and quiet in this neighborhood."

"I'll be a hermit until the book is finished," he warned.

"I understand, and if I don't see you again before you leave, I wish you the best of luck in getting the book published."

"Yeah . . . thanks." He stepped to the door and watched her step over the low hedge separating the drives.

Shae felt a little guilty about lying to her. After all,

they were adults now. He should have just leveled with her.

And what purpose would that have served other than to feed his inflated ego? There was no harm done. He would be back in New York in a few weeks, and Harriet would never suspect that he was Perry Beal.

If he told her, he knew how fast word traveled in a small town. She would tell everyone she knew, and there would go his privacy. And his work time.

"But I lied to her," he said out loud.

You didn't lie to her, he told himself, he just had not told the truth. Perry Beal was a pseudonym. She would never connect him with Perry Beal. After all, it was only Harriet—Harriet Whitlock? He *knew* what a pain Harriet could be.

Yes, he knew what a pain Harriet could be.

Boy, did he know what a pain Harriet could be.

Still, he couldn't shrug off the feeling that he should have been honest with her. She certainly seemed different.

Leaning against the door frame, his mind went back to their earlier conversation.

Patrick Mulligan and Harriet?

Damn. Mulligan could have had his pick of women, and he'd ended up with Harriet?

Straightening, he strained to get a final glimpse of her attractive backside as she disappeared into her parents' house.

Well, he supposed she could appeal to some men— under certain circumstances. Maybe a full moon, soft music, a little wine . . . a little insanity.

• • •

Shae was out of the house for a run early the next morning. He was halfway down the block when he glanced up to find Harri running along beside him.

"Good morning!"

Keeping his eyes straight ahead he grunted what he hoped she'd accept as an answer.

Her footsteps matched his as they jogged up a steep incline.

"I've been thinking about our conversation yesterday."

"Yeah?"

His eyes discreetly surveyed her attire. If she was trying to distract him with that thin little shirt and shorts she was wearing, it was working. She bounced in all the right places.

"If you need any help with that book you're writing, just let me know."

He glanced at her curiously. "Why? Do you write?"

"No, but I've read so many mysteries that I know fifty different ways to kill a person and get away with it."

"Yeah? So why don't you write a book of your own?"

They turned and headed up Main Street, their feet matching pace easily.

"I wouldn't be any good at writing, but I do know how to plot."

"Is that so." He wanted to participate in the conversation, but he was having trouble keeping pace with her.

"Yes, that's so." She stuck her tongue out playfully and pulled ahead, outdistancing him now by several feet.

Deciding that he wasn't going to let her beat him,

he increased his speed. They raced down the sidewalk, trying to pull ahead of each other.

By the time they reached Elinore's house, they were in a dead heat. Shae had to admit that she was in damn good shape.

Stopping on his lawn in exhaustion, he gasped for breath as she streaked past him. Over her shoulder, she called laughingly, "I hope you don't write like you run, Malone!"

Falling spread eagle on the lawn, he ignored her.

He didn't know how, but he was certain that she had cheated.

Harri took Florence back to the zoo with her that morning. She didn't want Magnolia to let the snake out of the cage again, and Florence was doing well enough to return to the zoo's population.

Harri had to admit that having Shae as a neighbor disturbed her. He'd always had his nose in the air where she was concerned, and though he had been polite this morning, she could tell he still had plenty of reservations about her.

Well, so what? She had a few of her own about him. In the future she planned to go out of her way to avoid him. The last thing she wanted to do was give him the impression that after all these years she was still interested in him.

"How about grabbing a burger after work?"

Harri glanced up from the reports she was typing to find Mike Stevenson smiling down at her.

Mike had been appointed director of the zoo when Denzil Matlock had had his third heart attack.

Mike was okay—a little overbearing at times, but

they were able to share an occasional dinner after work and not have it get in the way of professionalism.

"Sorry, I can't tonight, Mike. I have to mow my lawn."

"You can't procrastinate on that another day?"

Harri shook her head negatively. "It's nearly to the stage where I'll need a combine now."

"Then I'll let you grill me a hamburger tomorrow night."

"How thoughtful of you."

Grinning, Mike headed to the coffeepot to replenish his cup. "Heard you had a little trouble with Florence last night."

Sighing, Harri replied, "Magnolia let her out of the cage, again."

Ambling to Harri's desk, Mike took a sip of the coffee. "I don't suppose your neighbor was any too happy finding a python on his doorstep."

"No, but he was decent about it." Propping her elbows on the typewriter, Harri stared off thoughtfully. "Seems like Elinore Malone's grandson has decide to spend the summer in Cloverdale."

"Shae?"

"Yes, Shae . . . you know him?"

"Sure, he and I had a couple of classes together in junior high. What's ole Shae up to these days?"

"Attempting to write a book."

Mike's brows lifted skeptically. "A book?"

"Yes, can you imagine such a lofty goal?"

"Well, I don't know. Shae was always pretty sharp." Harri noticed Mike's eyes were twinkling with mischief as he winked at her. "Seems to me I remember that you had one humdinger of a crush on him."

Harri rolled her eyes, and her cheeks colored with

embarrassment. "Don't remind me. I made an absolute fool out of myself over him."

Mike's eyes met hers over the rim of his cup. "And now?"

"Now?"

"Now that you're all grown up, how does he strike you?"

"He strikes me as being a grump."

"No signs of the god you formerly had him pegged to be?"

"Not even a trace." She shrugged. "He's just a struggling writer, hoping to hit it big one of these days."

"And you're staying out of the donuts?"

She shot him an exasperated look. "Yes, I'm staying out of the donuts!"

It was a standing joke around the office that if Harri was upset about anything, someone would mercifully hide the donuts before she could begin an eating frenzy.

Chuckling, Mike started back to his office. "By the way, KWPT is sending a reporter to do a story on the picnic. I want you to do the interview," he called over his shoulder.

"Me! What time will they be here?"

"Around one."

"I wish someone would think to check with me before they make these appointments," she complained under her breath.

"You say something?"

"No," she glanced up, flashing Mike a pretty smile. "No problem. I can handle it."

When the door to Mike's office closed behind him,

she began typing with a vengeance, determined to put Shae Malone out of her mind.

She would not make a fool of herself over him, even if just seeing him again had cost her a night's sleep.

She had lain awake most of last night, tossing and turning, fighting to rid herself of the image of his sexy body and those preposterous blue eyes. Maybe this would be a good time to move to a larger zoo. She'd had offers recently from both San Diego and the Bronx—maybe after Mom and Dad returned it would be time to give the offers serious consideration. After all, she didn't plan to live in Cloverdale all her life.

And it was ridiculous for a grown woman to act this way over one very ordinary man. Well, she was in control again. She would just pretend that Elinore's house was *still* vacant.

Her parents would be back from Europe by the end of July, and she would return to her small three-room apartment on Millrose—a good twenty miles away from Sheridan Drive.

Satisfied to have that off her mind, she reached for a donut, stuck it in her mouth, and went back to typing.

Three

Shae was in his office staring at the computer screen late that afternoon, trying to block out the sound of the lawn mower running outside his window.

An occasional rock pinged against the side of the house, followed by a clod of dirt and flying grass.

Sighing, he stood up and stretched. There wasn't a chance he could concentrate with all that racket going on.

Looking outside the window, he saw Harri dragging the mower back and forth beneath a large snowball bush planted on the adjoining property line.

Allowing his eyes to travel leisurely over her tanned legs and trim derriere, he felt an unexpected tightening somewhere deep in his lower extremities. Appalled, he jerked his gaze away.

Easy, Malone. Don't be getting any crazy ideas. So all of a sudden Harriet Whitlock's developed a great tush. You know a lot of women with great tushes.

His eyes unwillingly strayed back to the short pair of navy blue running shorts and brief halter top she was wearing, and the tightening in his groin grew more pronounced.

Had she done something to enlarge her breasts or was she always that well-endowed?

He watched as she paused and reached up to tighten her headband. The stretchy fabric of her halter was strained.

Groaning, he restlessly shifted his stance, aware of where his thoughts could lead.

What was going on here? Fifteen years ago he ran like a jackrabbit from Harriet Whitlock. Now all of a sudden he was drooling over her from behind closed curtains? He was sick. Sick! He'd been working too hard.

Ducking, he flinched as another rock zinged toward the window, leaving a large imprint in the screen. After several attempts to rub the wrinkle out, he gave up.

Returning to the computer, he ran his hand over the back of his neck, staring at the screen.

He needed to get his mind back on his own work. And he needed to stop eyeing Harriet Whitlock as if he was a bull moose in heat.

Sitting down again, he typed another paragraph, listening to the mower chew up rocks and spit them out against the side of his house.

She *was* good-looking, he admitted to himself, but one thing was clear. She didn't know diddle squat about operating a lawn mower.

Ten minutes later, it also became clear that while his mind might be able to dismiss Harriet, his anatomy wasn't going to cooperate. Deciding to give it up, he flipped off the machine. He was consumed by an overwhelming urge for a cold shower and a long run.

After standing under the cold faucet for over twenty minutes, he left the shower and toweled off. He pulled on a pair of sweats and let himself out the back door a few minutes later.

When he spotted his red Corvette in the drive, he considered pulling it into the garage. The car had been washed and waxed that morning. Then glancing at the clear sky, he decided that he'd do it when he got back.

Harri spied him and waved. Lifting his hand, he gave her a casual salute. He paused just long enough to retie the front of his sweats before jogging off down the street.

Disappointed, Harri leaned against the mower. As she pushed her sweatband off her forehead, she watched the play of muscles in his tight buttocks.

Was anything worse than a red-headed, egotistical writer? Did he think he was bothering her?

Shoving the lawn mower back into action, she deliberately put Shae Malone out of her mind.

Elinore's house is empty, remember? There's nothing over there that interested her unless she'd suddenly developed a fetish for weeds and neglected pools.

Thirty minutes later, Harri finished mowing. Dragging the sprinkler to the side of the house, she connected it to the hose, then positioned it in the back yard.

As the screen door slammed behind her, Shae came jogging back around the corner. His sweats were drenched from the hard run, and his breath was coming in deep drafts.

Squatting down while he caught his breath, he experienced an unexplainable letdown when he noticed that Harri had disappeared. He was definitely losing it. First he'd run his butt off to get her off his mind, and then he was disappointed because she'd put him out of his misery.

Straightening, he walked up his drive, listening to the lazy drone of an oscillating sprinkler.

He stopped suddenly, his hands coming to his hips. There were puddles of water standing on the hood of the Corvette.

The sprinkler whished by again, drenching him.

Lifting his hand to wipe the water from his eyes, he glanced accusingly at Harri's bedroom window where he heard a feminine voice enthusiastically warbling a lively arpeggio in the shower. Shaking his head, his jaw firmed resentfully.

Harriet the Curse had struck again.

The following week they made a job of ignoring each other. Harri nodded pleasantly at Shae as she came out of her house each morning, and he nodded back at her.

Since they both jogged about the same time each day, she found it impossible to avoid him, but she refused to change her schedule. He wasn't on a time clock, so he could change his routine.

Though she wasn't keeping track, it seemed to her that the man was getting better looking every day. Although he wasn't tall, maybe five eight or nine, he was built.

Lord, was he built.

The morning that he returned from running wearing nothing but a pair of white shorts and blue Reeboks, Harri thought she was going to choke on the bite of toast she had just stuck into her mouth.

"What a bod!" Myron exclaimed as she nibbled on an orange slice.

"Yes, disgusting," Harri murmured, her eyes round as cup saucers as she gawked at the carpet of reddish-blond hair covering Shae's broad chest.

Deserting the window, she dumped the remains of her coffee into the sink, then put the cup in the dishwasher. "Magnolia!"

"Magnolia!" she called again when the monkey failed to appear. Squirting a blob of hand lotion in the palm of her hand, Harri massaged it into her hands.

"Myron, call Magnolia for me."

The bird rattled around in the bottom of its cage. "More orange, please."

"You've had enough orange."

"More orange, please."

"No."

"UP YOUR NOSE, MOOSE BREATH!"

Harri shook her head as she left the kitchen. THe bird's former trainer had had a strange sense of humor.

Magnolia wasn't in her usual position in front of the television, nor was she in the bedroom, Harri noticed as she gathered her purse and car keys.

Glancing at the clock on her night stand, she wondered if she should take the time to find her. She couldn't have wandered far. She had fed the monkey not ten minutes ago.

Well, she was around somewhere, Harri reasoned, and returned to the kitchen to fix a sandwich to take to work.

Next door, Shae anxiously watched the clock as he jerked his tie into place. He had overslept again, and by the time he had his run and showered, he was running late. A hurried glance in the mirror told him that however he looked would have to do.

He grabbed his briefcase and bounded down the stairway, taking two steps at a time, grabbing a powdered donut from a box on the kitchen table on his way out.

Driving to the city to meet with his attorney was not his favorite way to start the day, but the movie rights to *Murder, She Cried* were being commissioned, and he wanted a say in the script.

Jamming the donut into his mouth, he slipped behind the wheel of the Corvette and inserted the key into the ignition. The engine sprang to life.

He shifted into reverse and roared out of the garage. At that instant, a fur ball leaped from behind the seat and grabbed him around the face, holding on with a death-like grip.

The donut crumbled down the front of his suit as Shae tried to fight off his attacker. Claws imbedded themselves into his face like knife points as he stomped the floor, searching for the brake pedal.

The car shot wildly down the drive accompanied by the squeal of rubber and Shae's astounded shouts. While he fought the steering wheel with one hand, he grabbed for the hairy object with the other, trying to pry it off his face.

Shae felt claws gouging his eyes, blocking his vision as he struggled to retain control of the car. Dumbfounded, he felt the wheels slam over the curb and head for a row of shrubs lining the drive. Finally, his flailing foot managed to locate the brake.

Harri was mixing tuna when all the commotion started. Puzzled by the shriek of tires and man, she leaned over the sink and stared, gasping as she saw the scene taking place outside her window.

Taking a deep breath, she clamped her eyes shut, bracing herself as she heard the Corvette slice through the line of shrubs connecting the drives, and come to a sudden, screeching halt.

"Oh, Lord," she murmured as an uneasy calm descended, then she quickly braced herself again as Shae's irate voice shattered the early morning stillness.

"HARRIET WHITLOCK! GET YOUR BUTT OUT HERE!"

With a sigh of resignation, Harri glanced at the lion cub lying on the floor chewing on a rubber bone. Sheepishly, she said, "You can see why he wants to be a writer. The man really knows how to express himself."

As Harri tiptoed toward the Corvette, she saw that Shae was still sitting behind the wheel with Magnolia clutching his neck. He looked dazed and shaken, not sure yet what had just happened.

Leaning her elbow on the car window, Harri gazed at him evenly. "You bellowed?"

"Is this your monkey?"

"Well, not mine—"

His hand shot up impatiently. "I know, I know.

She's not yours, but let me guess—you're responsible for her, right?"

"Right."

"Then would you kindly get her off my neck!"

Harri calmly reached into the car to remove the monkey. "Magnolia, come here."

Ignoring the command, the monkey clung to Shae's neck possessively.

"Magnolia," Harri warned, trying to stifle the giggle that threatened to overcome her. The situation wasn't funny—yet the look on Shae's face *was*.

"I can't believe you find this entertaining."

"I know—I'm sorry." She tried to contain her amusement, but it kept coming out in a sort of strangled snort. "Magnolia's on medication that makes her hyper."

Harri opened the door to the Corvette and gently pried the monkey's hands loose from Shae's forehead. "I think she likes you," she offered, trying to put the best gloss she could on the humiliating incident.

"Wonderful. That's all I need," Shae was fuming as he stepped out of the car and knocked the donut crumbs off the front of his suit, "an amorous monkey living next door."

Harri blocked another snort when she saw the layer of powdered sugar rimming his mouth.

"Stop being such a grump. I said I was sorry."

Shae groaned as he spotted the long, angry scratch running down the door panel. "Just look at that!"

Frowning, Harri said meekly, "I have insurance."

Shae knelt to run his hand along the deep scratch. It took a supreme effort for him to remain civil.

It was bad enough having to live next door to a

female Marlon Perkins, but when her animals seized control of his car, *that's* where he drew the line!

"Don't worry about the shrubs," Harri murmured.

His pointed glance assured her he wasn't concerned in the least about the shrubs.

"If you'll just step inside, I'll give you the name of my insurance company."

Shae stood up and dusted off his hands. "I'll have to call a tow truck and have it lift my car out of these bushes. I don't want it scratched anymore than it already is."

"You can use my phone." By this time she would've built him a Titan missile if it would have made him feel any better.

He glanced at the scratch again. "I'll need to call my lawyer."

Harri tensed, gathering Magnolia to her protectively. "Your lawyer? Isn't that a little drastic?"

Shae sighed as he ran his hand over the back of his neck. "We had an appointment this morning." Glancing at his watch, he added in a strained tone, "Obviously, I'm not going to make it."

Shifting Magnolia to her hip, Harri turned and started for the house, trying to hide the color that had suddenly flooded her face. She didn't know why, but whenever she was around him, she invariably looked like an idiot.

"They'll never be able to match the paint." His lower lip practically dragged the ground as he trailed dejectedly behind her.

"The car's new, isn't it?"

"Yes, but that doesn't make any difference. Once they start messing around with the paint, it never looks the same."

Entering the house by a side door, Harri carried Magnolia into the kitchen and placed her back into her cage.

Harri was sorry that his car had been scratched, but she had little patience with his gloomy observations. The paint didn't match anywhere on the '72 Volkswagen she drove.

Starting around him, she paused long enough to pick a stray remnant of donut from the front of his shirt.

"Want a cup of coffee to go with this?"

For the first time she saw just a trace of the Shae Malone she knew existed. The faintest hint of a smile touched the corners of his mouth as he shrugged. "Hell, why not?"

"The phone's over there." She motioned toward the living room as she moved to the coffee maker. "Cream or sugar?"

"Light, no sugar."

While Harri poured coffee, Shae made the calls. When he noticed the paperback copy of *Murder, She Cried* lying on the floor next to the chintz-covered chair, he called into the kitchen to her.

"I thought you were a fan of Perry Beal."

"I am! Why?"

"Are you too cheap to buy a hardback copy of his book?"

"Are you kidding? At eighteen ninety-five a copy?"

Eyeing the large bird perched in a cage next to the sofa, Shae edged away to stand closer to the end table as he waited for the operator to put his credit-card call through to New York. The bird seemed to be fascinated with him, and it only added to Shae's discomfort.

Harri appeared in the doorway holding two mugs of coffee as he finished speaking with his lawyer's secretary and hung up.

Handing one of the mugs to him, she smiled. "Did you call the garage?"

"Yeah, it'll take fifteen to twenty minutes to get a tow truck over here."

"Oh—well, I guess I should call Mike."

Their hands brushed as Shae took the cup from her. The way her pulse started thumping reminded Harri of the vibration she felt when a tire on her Volkswagen had gone flat.

Shae's left brow lifted. "Mike?"

"My boss—Mike Stevenson. He mentioned that the two of you knew each other in junior high."

Harri deliberately ignored the annoying twitch in her stomach that occurred each time Shae looked directly at her. She couldn't remember Patrick—or any other man—having the same, disarming effect on her.

Harri, really. He doesn't *look any better in that expensive three piece business suit than any other man. And his eyes* aren't *any bluer or brighter or any more arresting than any other man with blue eyes.*

And just ignore the way his hair—all freshly washed and blown dry—curls around the nape of his neck.

Handle his sexy after-shave the same way. Remember that the masculine, spicy scent is supposed to drive a woman up the wall. It's meant to warn a woman that this man is a risk taker, an adventurer touched by wanderlust.

"Mike? Sure, I know Mike," Shae was saying. "He's with the zoo now?"

"Yes, he was appointed director when Denzil Matlock retired."

"Mike Stevenson? I thought he wanted to be a doctor."

"He did, but after his dad died, money became tight. When Mike finished college, he took a job with the zoo to help support his mom and two younger sisters."

Shae watched her closely as he took a sip of his coffee. "Is he still as obnoxious as ever?"

Dropping her gaze, Harri chose her words carefully. "Mike doesn't have any trouble expressing himself—but he's good at his job," she was quick to add.

Shae was looking at her again, still sizing her up, actually, and it annoyed her.

"When did you cut your hair?"

Harri's self-consciously touched the short layered cut she had worn for the past couple of years. "A long time ago."

He was only a few inches taller than she, and for some reason Harri found that sexy. If a miracle were to occur to cause him to draw her into his arms, everything would match up nicely; all the right things touching in all the right places.

Shae continued to study her sporty, flattering cut, and she couldn't tell if he approved of it or not. With him, you could never be quite sure.

"It's a definite improvement over those tail things you used to wear."

The memory of her pig tails brought a smile to her

face. "They were awful, weren't they? Mother made me wear them."

"Did she make you wear those horrible glasses, too?"

He knew he wasn't being very tactful, but she wasn't wearing glasses now. Obviously, she had gone to contact lenses.

Setting her mug on the table, Harri again chose her words prudently. "You know, Shae, I always had the impression that it wouldn't have made any difference to you what I wore when we were in junior high."

It was the first time the subject had been broached, and she wasn't sure how he would react. There was the faintest glint of humor in his eyes now. "Well, I have to admit, Harriet, you've changed."

"In what way?" She was determined to wring at least one concession out of him before she drew her last breath.

Letting the subject slide, Shae motioned toward the bird cage beside the sofa. "What's wrong with the bird?"

"Myron? He has a stomach disorder. You'll find him loud-mouthed, nosy, and downright pious at times, but he's harmless."

"Another orange, please."

Harri shook her head warningly at the bird, hoping Myron would take no for an answer and not cause a scene. "You've had enough orange."

"More orange, please."

Harri shook her head again. "No more orange."

"Well, up yours, cupcake!"

Harri glanced at Shae and blushed. "You'll have to

excuse his vocabulary—he belonged to a very strange trainer before he was donated to the zoo."

The corners of Shae's mouth lifted with amusement. "I'm surprised to find you working with animals. Somehow I had the impression you would end up marrying right out of high school."

"No, I went to college. Somehow, and don't ask me why, I ended up with a degree in wildlife management and conservation. After graduation, I came home to visit my parents for a few days, and Denzil Matlock called and offered me a job as zookeeper of the reptiles.

"I'll admit that at first I accepted the job on a temporary basis—just until I could decide where I wanted to settle. Then Patrick and I started dating, and after a whirlwind courtship, we were married." She studied the rim of her cup thoughtfully. "When Patrick died of an aneurysm two years ago, I thought about leaving," she glanced up and sighed, "but by then Denzil had had his third heart attack. Mike took over as director, and he encouraged me to stay on as his assistant. I've spent the last year and a half handling marketing, education, volunteer programs, and public relations."

"Was Patrick still involved in football?"

"Yes, he'd just signed to play with the Denver Broncos. He took a hard blow to the head one day in practice . . . he died twelve hours later in the emergency room."

"That had to be rough on you."

"Yes, it was rough on everyone who loved him," she admitted. "Patrick's parents are still devastated."

Shae glanced at the various cages set around the

room. "How many animals do you have here with you?"

"Just Magnolia and Myron and Florence—oh, you'll be relieved to hear that Florence is back at the zoo."

Harri noticed Myron seemed unusually preoccupied with Shae, and it made her uneasy. She never knew what was going to come out of the bird's mouth.

Mynahs were known to rival parrots in their power to mimic human speech, and the man who had previously owned the bird had been an uninhibited navy man with the most sordid vocabulary.

"You might as well make yourself comfortable," she said as she headed back to the kitchen to refill their cups. "The truck won't be here for another ten minutes."

"Thanks." Shae moved to the sofa and absently shoved aside a stuffed animal as he sat down.

The toy suddenly sprang upright, snapping at him.

Springing back to his feet, Shae felt the coffee spill down the side of his trousers as he lunged to get away from the lion cub.

"Oh—and Ricky," Harri added belatedly. Smiling apologetically, Harri removed the dripping cup from his hand and handed him a napkin.

Shae sopped at the coffee on his trousers, eyeing Ricky resentfully. "How do you live like this?"

Leaning down, Harri retrieved the cub and ruffled his fur affectionately. "You get used to it. Ricky has rickets."

"In addition to sharp teeth," Shae added.

Giving the cub an affectionate squeeze, Harri placed him back on the sofa. "Ricky's former owner fed him a steady diet of hamburgers, spaghetti, and tacos."

"What's wrong with that?"

"Nothing—if you want a case of rickets. Cats can't eat what humans eat. They need a special diet of raw meat and vitamins." She scratched behind the cub's ears playfully. "Ricky is almost ready to return to the zoo. We've just finished building a special place that will allow him to be outside part of the time. It's unfair to always keep an animal caged."

"That's how I prefer them."

Her brow lifted. "You don't like animals?"

"I don't know. I've never been around one that much."

She cocked her head skeptically. "Surely you had a dog or a cat when you were growing up."

"No, I didn't. I'm city born and bred. They didn't allow animals in the apartment where we lived. And even if they had, my parents traveled a lot. There was never time or space to have a pet."

"That's sad." Harri assumed everyone had owned a pet at least once in his life. "I've had animals since I was a baby—turtles, rabbits, dogs, cats."

"Well, I didn't."

"Not even a goldfish?"

"Not even a goldfish." Shae glanced at his watch. "That truck should have been here by now."

Harri racked her brain for a more stimulating topic to discuss. "How's the book coming along?"

"Slow."

"Well." She reached for a sheet of paper lying on the end table. "I've jotted down a couple of ideas you might want to think about.

Glancing up, his features softened. "Harri . . . I appreciate it, but it isn't necessary—"

"I don't mind, really. You don't have to use them, but I wish you'd at least look at them."

Harri handed him the sheet as she heard the tow truck pull into the drive. "It sounds like the cavalry has arrived."

He folded the paper and stuck it into his pocket, then followed her to the back door.

As she brushed past him, he caught the faint scent of her perfume. The light, floral scent was oddly distracting.

"Excuse me—"

"No, go right ahead—"

A small, elderly man wearing a New York Mets baseball cap was standing in the drive looking at the Corvette as they came out of the house.

"Hi, Charlie," Harri called.

"Mornin', Ms. Whitlock. Looks like you got yourself a real peck of trouble." Charlie shoved the cap back on his forehead as he stepped back to evaluate the scratch running down the right side of the car. "Yep, got yourself a real mess, all right."

"Can you get the car out of there without doing any further damage?" Shae asked, eyeing the prickly shrubs apprehensively.

Charlie scratched his chin thoughtfully. "Might— can't promise nothing though."

Stepping closer, Harri murmured out of the corner of her mouth, "Try hard, Charlie."

Fifteen minutes later, the Corvette was sitting back in the drive.

Shae walked around the car looking for scratches as Harri signed the bill.

"Hate to charge so much, Ms. Whitlock, but you got to handle them sports cars like rotten eggs," Charlie said.

"Don't worry about it, Charlie. I'm hoping that my insurance covers it." Harri surveyed the bill glumly. If it didn't, there went the winter coat she had been saving for months to buy.

Charlie climbed back inside his truck and eased it out of the drive. "If you need anything else, just holler!"

Harri waved back. "Sure will. Thanks, Charlie."

Shae climbed into the Corvette as Harri started back up the drive. "Everything all right?"

"I don't know—seems to be."

He started the engine and let it idle for a moment. "Shae."

He glanced up. "Yes?"

As always, she was reluctant to let him go. "I'm sorry—I hope your lawyer isn't upset about your being late."

"If he is, he'll get over it." He smiled.

She paused, trying to find enough courage to ask him over for dinner that evening. She had never asked a man to dinner before. She had never wanted to until now.

Discretion, Harri, she told herself. If she was going to do this, she would handle it with finesse and complete discretion.

Shae slipped the car into gear and turned back to face her. "Thanks for the use of your phone."

Stepping back, Harri's courage failed her. She couldn't ask him.

"Sure—anytime." She watched as he backed out of the drive, then sped off down the street.

She was a chicken—a big chicken. Why didn't she just ask him? The worst he could have said was no.

Which he would have, a voice in her head reminded.

Sighing, she went back into the house where she picked up her purse, the Perry Beal novel, and her car keys, wishing she'd had the nerve to ask him. It would have been nicer if he'd asked her, but she didn't plan to hold her breath until he did.

She wasn't blind. He found her attractive, but he was still leery of her.

But she wasn't the same imperious, domineering Harriet Whitlock who'd terrorized him in junior high. Somehow she had to find a way to make him see that.

"Hi."

"Hi."

Shae glanced down to find Harri running beside him again the next morning. His gaze lazily assessed the red tank top she was wearing.

The gentle rain had formed the shirt snugly to her breasts. Her slim, tanned legs matched his long strides, and Shae felt his body begin to respond to hers. Glancing away hurriedly, he sincerely hoped that she wouldn't notice.

"Have you had time to look at my ideas?"

"Yeah, I took a look at them." He'd taken a long look. Though she claimed no interest in writing, her ideas were good. Damn good for a novice. He was surprised. And impressed.

"Well, what do you think?"

"Not bad."

She glanced over, flashing him an expectant grin. "Really? You liked them?"

They crossed the street, and started up Main.

"They've got possibilities."

"Even the part about the heroine falling in love with the butler?"

"Strange twist, but it could work," he conceded.

"Well, I realize I haven't actually seen your manuscript, but from what little you've told me I was hoping you might want to use some of the concepts."

"Harri, the first thing you learn as a writer is that you don't give away material," he said.

"But I'm not a writer, and I never want to be."

They turned the corner, and picked up speed.

"Please, use anything you like. I have lots more ideas where those came from."

"I couldn't use your material. It would be unethical."

She flashed him another grin. "Chicken. You just said they had possibilities, and I just gave you my permission to use them."

"What's in it for you?"

"Nothing, I just want to see you get published." She began to pull ahead of him again, and he knew what was coming. "Not that you deserve it, but let's just say I'm a nice person," she called over her shoulder.

Shae tried to pick up speed; she was running a good ten feet ahead of him now. They flew down the street, competing against each other. Her infectious laughter spurred him on, but she was small and had the advantage on the corners.

Collapsing in a heap on his lawn a few minutes

later, he watched as she blew past him, throwing a victory kiss as she sprinted lithely up her drive. Grinning, he rolled onto his back, letting the light rain wash over his flushed face.

Damn, he was going to get her one of these days.

Four

"There he is, men! Shoot him down like the filthy dog he is!"

The sound of galloping horses, frenzied shouts, and sporadic gunfire caused Shae to sit straight up out of a sound sleep early Saturday morning.

Cowering, he listened as bullets whizzed by his head, then ricocheted across the room.

Who was shooting? Oh Lord, *his head!* Had he been hit? There was an excruciating pain now, just above his left sinus.

Struggling to clear his mind, his gaze darted to the clock on the mantle. Seven-fifteen. He'd slept only two hours.

When he had finally called it a night and collapsed on the sofa for a couple hours sleep, the sun had just begun to peek over the rim of the horizon. The book had finally started to roll, and he had been so engrossed in the story, he had lost all track of time.

Lifting his head again, he listened to the sound of

horses galloping down the hallway. Guns blazed, and hoofbeats bounced off the walls.

Rolling off the sofa, he groped for support as the afghan wrapped around his legs, pitching him onto the floor.

Struggling to his feet, he banged his head against the edge of the coffee table as a gun fired again.

His hand shot up to search for blood, praying the second bullet had only grazed him. He felt a flood of relief when his hand came away clean.

The gunfire continued as he started crawling down the hallway on his belly, keeping his head low to the floor. It suddenly dawned on him that the noise was coming from his bedroom. As the fog lifted even more, he realized that the racket wasn't an intruder, but that the noise was coming from the portable television setting on top of the chest of drawers.

Pausing in front of the doorway, he squinted around the pain in his forehead, his eyes searching. Spotting nothing unusual, he crawled farther into the room.

By now, he could see the lounger next to his bed. His heart nearly stopped beating when he discovered that there was someone sitting in it.

Craning his neck, he viewed an uncommonly hairy back. What now? He was unarmed. He should have thought to grab a vase or an umbrella from the stand in the hallway before coming in here.

From his vantage point, he couldn't make out the size of the man—no woman would allow herself to become that hairy—but he supposed it didn't matter. He'd just have to gut it out and hope that he was bigger. After crawling to the bed, he eased himself up to peer over the top of the mattress.

His eyes widened, then narrowed in disbelief when he spotted the source of trouble. Magnolia sat with her eyes glued to Hoss Cartright, a grim-faced sheriff, Pa, Adam, and Little Joe as they galloped their horses across the nineteen-inch screen in hot pursuit of three men wearing large, black hats and riding swift mounts.

"Magnolia!" Shae bellowed, springing to his feet irritably.

Magnolia glanced up, her eyes growing round at the sound of an irate voice.

Shae bound across the bed to snatch his remote control from the monkey's hand. "Give me that! How did you get in here?"

Magnolia's innocent orbs drifted to the small opening in the wall beside the double french doors leading onto the flagstone patio.

"Zoomer," Shae muttered, realizing immediately what had happened.

Elinore had installed a dog door to allow her pet boxer to come and go as he pleased. That pet door would have to be replaced immediately.

Shrugging into his jeans and a shirt, Shae padded barefoot toward the kitchen, wondering how long it was going to take Harri to figure out that one of her animals was on the loose again.

Magnolia came along, hitching a ride on his leg.

"Hey, look . . . I can't walk with you hanging onto my leg," he complained.

He paused to pry the monkey's hands loose, but found his efforts were useless.

"Okay, you win. At least until I down a quart of caffeine."

Entering the kitchen, he spotted the aspirin bottle. His head was throbbing as he removed the lid, and shook out a couple of tablets. He tossed them into his mouth and took a swallow of water, then reached for the coffee pot.

When the pot was filled, he plugged it in, then shot a squirt of nasal spray up each nostril.

Glancing resentfully at the clock again, he mumbled something about how he didn't appreciate having his home turned into an animal house.

Magnolia chirped and scrambled up to his shoulder as he turned to the refrigerator. He pulled the door open and shoved aside remnants of pizza, containers of beef broccoli, eggrolls, Crab Rangoon, chop suey, and two packages whose contents bore a vague but repulsive resemblance to soggy french fries and four "spicy" chicken winglets wrapped in a paper towel.

Finally, he located the package of bacon.

Walking over to the box of pots and pans that was still waiting to be unpacked, he rummaged around until he found a skillet. A few minutes later, the smell of sizzling bacon drifted pleasantly through the open kitchen window.

Cheating, he reached for his cup and stuck it beneath the drip of the coffee maker, weary of waiting for the pot to fill.

He glanced at the ball of fur perched on his shoulder. His gaze was met by two inquisitive, beady brown orbs. "Why can't you attach yourself to something else . . . like maybe the table leg or a fast freight on its way out of town?"

Magnolia calmly reached out and placed one of her fingers on his nose and mashed down.

"Bug off, will you?" Shae demanded in a nasal tone.

Taking a sip of coffee, he wondered again how he had ever let his dad talk him into coming back to Cloverdale. If the interruptions continued, he wouldn't have a prayer of finishing the book on time.

Harri popped into his mind, and he shrugged the image aside.

One of these days he was going to have to tell her that he was Perry Beal—especially now that she had developed this thing about wanting to help him write the book.

Moving to the counter, he removed the loaf of bread from the cabinet, and popped a couple of slices into the toaster. The time had come for him to put his foot down with Harri Whitlock. He certainly couldn't let her help him write the book. And she was either going to keep her animals under control, or he was going to demand that they go back to the zoo where they belonged.

And if she tried to give him any flak, he'd just remind her that he wasn't above calling the zoning commission to see what they thought about citizens being forced to share quarters with pythons or monkeys with crushes. Let her see what they'd have to say about that.

Magnolia chirped indignantly as if she could read his thoughts and resented them.

Shae calmly lifted his cup to his mouth, ignoring the monkey's incessant chatter. "Nothing personal, Maggie ole girl, but that's the way it is."

• • •

Harri paused before rapping on Shae's back door, trying to catch her breath.

The fragrant aroma of bacon overpowered the scent of Elinore's American Beauty roses trailing up a wooden trellis beside the porch.

Harri prayed she was mistaken, but she knew there was little hope of that. When she had discovered Magnolia missing again, she'd known instinctively where to look for her.

For some reason the animals seemed to gravitate to this man.

First Florence, then Magnolia and the car incident, and now Magnolia was very likely over here bothering him again.

Drawing another deep breath, Harri rapped briskly on the window pane.

The door swung open to reveal a rumpled and decidedly grumpy Shae.

Harri flashed him a helpless smile, staring back at a pair of bloodshot eyes that bore a vague resemblance to a road map in her glove compartment.

"Hi . . . me again," she said lamely.

"Ms. Whitlock, how good of you to call."

"Why, thank you, Mr. Malone. It's always nice to see you looking so chipper." Harri forced back a grin. His lovely red hair was matted on one side, and standing straight up in the back. "I hate to ask, but . . ." Her words wavered as she began to grin in spite of herself. It was impossible to keep a straight face when confronted with such a monumental case of bed head.

"Do you find something amusing?" he asked.

Hurriedly straightening her features, she shook her head. "No—did I awaken you?"

"No, *you* didn't." Following the direction of his gaze, Harri spotted Magnolia peeking out from behind the calf of his left leg.

"Oh, dear."

Holding the door open wider, Shae sighed. "You might as well come in. I'm wide awake, now."

Harri stepped into the kitchen, and Shae handed her a cup of coffee. "Had breakfast, yet?"

"No . . . I've been too busy looking for her," Harri admitted, sending a stern look in Magnolia's direction.

"Well, as usual, she's attached to me." He gave her a look of strained tolerance. "I'll give you everything I own to pry her off my leg."

Harri set her cup on the table and bent down to cluck to Magnolia, who reluctantly came into her arms.

"Harri, I mean it, you're going to have to do something about this," Shae warned.

"I know . . . and I know you think I do a miserable job of caring for the animals, but I do my best to keep them out of your hair . . ."

Her voice faded as she recalled the comical picture of Magnolia perched on top of his head the day his car landed in the bushes.

Shae turned back to the stove and began to dish up scrambled eggs, bacon, on separate plates.

"I don't like to complain, but you're going to have to either keep them under control or take them back to the zoo. Thanks to our little friend here, I only got a couple hours sleep."

"I'm sorry, and it won't happen again. They'll all be back in the zoo within a month," she promised.

Shae mumbled something under his breath that

she couldn't quite catch, and decided she didn't want to hear.

"How're things going?" she asked, hoping to change the subject.

"You mean the book?"

"Yes."

"I don't know . . . you don't seriously think I could convince the reader that the murder was committed with a hair pin, do you?"

"Of course—think about it. Have you read a mystery where the victim was poisoned by using the tip of a hair pin?"

"No," he said slowly, "shouldn't that tell you something?"

She smiled, reaching into her pocket to draw out another sheet of paper.

He groaned when he saw that it contained more ideas on how to plot.

"Just look at them—you don't have to use them verbatim."

After accepting the sheet of paper, he laid it aside.

"I'll bet you're good." she ventured.

He turned to hand her a plate, and their eyes met. "I can be."

The suggestive tone of his voice sent her pulse thumping, but she refused to acknowledge the effect he had on her. "May I read your work sometime?"

"No, I never let anyone read my work until it's finished."

"You think it's bad luck?"

He retrieved the bread from the toaster and buttered two slices, deciding a change of subject was in order. "You work on Saturdays?"

"No, not as a rule, but I promised Mike I would lend him a hand today."

Slipping a chain around Magnolia's neck, Harri tied the other end to the leg of a chair, relieved that the newest crisis was over without bloodshed. "Do you mind if I wash my hands?"

Shae motioned towards the sink. "The paper towels are in the cabinet below."

After she'd dried her hands, they sat down at Elinore's round oak table and began to eat.

Ordinarily, Harri would have felt nervous about sharing a meal with a man for the first time, but this morning she just felt hungry. She supposed it was because this particular man had made it obvious that he didn't consider her as a "woman" but rather as a necessary evil that he was condemned to tolerate.

Tackling her meal with a healthy appetite, Harri buttered her toast again, then reached for the strawberry jam. "I suppose a writer doesn't have a day off."

"No, not really." Shae watched as she scooped out two large spoonfuls of jam and smeared them on the bread. He'd never eaten breakfast with a woman who put jam on her toast.

Women he'd dated never allowed themselves the luxury of eating breakfast, or if they did, they would nibble on half a grapefruit and sip endless cups of black coffee while they eyed his eggs and bacon with hostility.

"This is very good."

"Thank you." Shae reached for the jam before she finished it off. Would she be as relaxed on a dinner date, he wondered. Now wouldn't that be something?

Take a woman to dinner, spend fifty dollars a plate, and have her actually eat the food?

"I'm sorry Magnolia bothered you again. I plan to talk to Mike this morning and see if we can't come up with a different arrangement until the new building is finished."

"You and Mike see each other on a personal basis?" Shae asked casually.

"Occasionally—this jam is wonderful," she said, reaching for the jar again.

Shae had a guilty look on his face as he got up to retrieve the coffee pot. "Thanks . . . I made it."

Surprised, Harri paused, holding a knife in mid-air. "You make your own jam?"

Shrugging, he filled her cup, his look openly daring her to make something of it. "All you have to do is take those green things off the berries, dump in a couple of cups of sugar, add this stuff called Reliable Jell, then pour it into jars and stick them in the freezer. It tastes better than what you buy at the market."

"I agree. I just never met a man who makes his own jam."

"It isn't like I can green beans or anything," he said defensively.

"I know . . . there's nothing wrong with a man making jam." She dipped her spoon into the jar again to prove it. "It's really very good."

"Just don't go spreading it around the neighborhood that Shae Malone makes his own jelly," he said. He wondered why he had told her in the first place.

She raised her hand solemnly. "My lips are sealed."

He stared at her sourly. "Your lips also have strawberry jam on them."

She picked up her napkin and wiped her mouth, glad that she wasn't trying to impress him. As usual, she hadn't come close.

They ate in silence for a moment, then he asked, "Why do you have to go in to work this morning?"

"The zoo is planning a picnic to raise the additional funds we need to finish the remodeling project. I promised Mike I would help with the last minute details." Harri glanced up from her plate. "Why don't you come to the picnic?"

"No, thanks." Shae didn't have time for picnics anymore. All his time was taken up with either trying to finish one book or start a new one.

"Well, it's none of my business, but from what I've seen, you work too hard. A little relaxation would do you good. If you came to the picnic, you would have the opportunity to meet a few of your neighbors."

Harri knew he had kept himself almost a recluse since he'd been back. "As small as Cloverdale is, everyone will be there."

Shae stared at the cup he was holding, realizing he had forgotten how to relax. "Sorry, but I really can't spare the time."

"Why not?"

He glanced up. He wasn't accustomed to having to explain his actions. Usually people were in awe of him—or perhaps his profession. He was never quite sure, but they never questioned him. "I'm trying to meet a deadline."

She frowned. "Whose deadline?"

He caught himself. "My deadline—if I don't set deadlines, I don't get anything done."

"Sometimes your mind works better if you give it a rest." She picked up her napkin and wiped her mouth, then pushed herself back from the table. "And besides that, I'm stuck with fifty tickets that I have to sell by the end of next week."

Shae grinned. In spite of himself, he was beginning to like her. He felt an ease with her that he couldn't explain, and the feeling was getting stronger every time they were together. He wondered if she felt it too.

Did he have this comfortable, relaxed, old-shoe feeling because she was unaware that he was Perry Beal, the mystery writer?

Shae was proud of his success—he'd worked damn hard to earn it—yet it was good to be just Shae Malone in a woman's eyes again. He hadn't enjoyed that privilege in a long time. Sometimes he wondered if he still had what it took to attract a woman without the added lure of his success. Especially a woman as attractive and intelligent as Harri.

He reached for another piece of toast and bit into it thoughtfully.

Up to now he'd been keeping his identity from her because he didn't like the thought of her chasing him again, but now. . . . He studied her out of the corner of his eye, fascinated by the turn of his thoughts.

Would she find him attractive, interesting . . . even sexy if he kept her in the dark indefinitely about his success? Shae found the possibility mildly intriguing.

"So?" she asked.

He glanced up, the toast still stuck in his mouth, surprised to find her staring at him. "So, what?"

His gaze centered with fascination on the dimple

that appeared, then disappeared at the corner of her mouth as she talked. "So, how many tickets will you take off my hands?"

"How much are they?"

Harri winced, remembering that he was a struggling writer, and money was probably scarce. "Three dollars—but I was only kidding about you buying tickets. If you want to come, I'll pay your way."

Shae's brows lifted in skepticism. No woman had offered to buy him anything lately, with the exception of his mother. "You'll buy my ticket?"

"Sure." She surveyed his hair and bloodshot eyes, and she smiled. He looked like a very tired little boy who could use a hot dog and a cold slice of watermelon. "Want to come?"

Shae found himself wanting to accept her offer. Not because he had any particular interest in the picnic, but because he wanted to be with her. "I don't know, Harri. I'd like to, but I'm not getting anything done." Disappointment replaced her sunny smile, and he hurriedly tried to soften the rejection. "But I'll see what I can do."

"I know you're busy, and if you let yourself, you'll end up talking yourself out of it. Just make up your mind to go, and do it," she urged.

He grinned. "I'll see how the book is coming by then. When is it?"

"Saturday, and of course I'll expect you to pay me back once 'the book' hits the best-seller list." She flashed him a cheeky grin.

He felt another rush of guilt as he stood up, letting the remark pass. He watched as she moved across the room to unchain Magnolia. Lifting the monkey into her arms, she turned and smiled again. "Thanks for the breakfast. It was delicious."

Shae walked to the freezer and pulled out a jar of strawberry jam. He didn't know why, but he suddenly wanted to do something personal for her. "Here, take this with you."

"Are you sure? I'll pay you for it?" she offered as he walked her to the door. She was sure he could use a little extra money.

"No, you can bake me some cookies someday."

"Sure—what kind?"

"Oatmeal—with raisins and plenty of nuts."

"You got it. And my back door is always open if you need to borrow anything when I'm not there."

He frowned. "Isn't that a dangerous habit, leaving your doors unlocked?"

"Maybe in Manhattan, but not in Cloverdale."

They reached the doorway, and paused. "Well, thanks again, and I'm sorry about Magnolia getting you out of bed so early."

Shae leaned against the doorway, allowing his gaze to roam leisurely over the blue tee shirt she had carelessly thrown on before coming over this morning. The way she dressed was slowly driving him crazy.

"Why don't you buy yourself some decent shirts?"

"Why? What's wrong with the ones I wear?"

Harri knew the fabric was too thin and that it revealed a little too much, but that's why she'd worn it. Just for him.

"You don't work in those things, do you?"

"No."

There was a chemistry between them. She could feel it, and her insides turned to the same consistency as the jam she was holding when she realized he was feeling it too.

There was a deeper significance to their visual exchange. He liked what he saw.

"Have you done something?" His eyes motioned to the front of her shirt.

She cocked her brow. "Really, Shae."

"I guess that wasn't very diplomatic . . . I just don't remember you looking like this when we were younger."

"I wasn't like this . . . when we were younger."

Their gazes suddenly refused to leave one another's, and as she absently released her hold on Magnolia, the monkey slid down the leg of her jeans.

"I noticed an ice cream parlor on the corner of Elm and Metcalf," he said.

"Yes, I walk down there for a chocolate cone nearly every night."

His eyes ran lazily over her full bottom lip, his thoughts ill-concealed now. "I'm partial to chocolate. Why don't you give me a call next time you go, and we'll walk down together."

"Sure, why not?" Harri was sure he could hear her heart trying to hammer its way out of her chest. "I suppose I'll have to buy the ice cream too?"

"No, I can probably scrape up enough to buy a couple of cones—what do a couple of cones cost these days?"

"A couple of dollars."

"A couple of dollars, huh?"

She nodded. "Too much?"

He shrugged. "I can swing it."

Magnolia chirped, and began to shimmy up Shae's

pant leg. Reaching his shoulder, the monkey began to hop around excitedly.

Shae turned to the animal reluctantly. "Are you back?"

Magnolia began chattering, trying to nudge Shae's head forward. He glanced at Harri. "What's she want?"

Harri blushed. She knew what Magnolia wanted, but she was too embarrassed to tell him.

The monkey persisted, batting at Shae's head purposefully, trying to force his head closer to Harri's. Puzzled, Shae glanced back to Harri, and she started to laugh. "She wants you to kiss me."

"Kiss you?"

She nodded, reaching for the monkey again. "Come here, Magnolia!"

Harri had to admit that she was a little disappointed when the monkey gave in so easily. "It's a game Mike's taught her," she apologized. "After I clean Magnolia's cage, Mike rewards me with a kiss."

Shae's face sobered. "A kiss?"

"Yes, you know Mike—"

"Yes, I do know Mike," he said coolly. "He likes the skirts."

"What man doesn't? Anyway, Magnolia picked up on the playful gesture, and now she thinks anyone I'm with is obligated to kiss me."

Turning, she started out the door when Shae's hand suddenly reached out to block her. "Hold on a minute."

Pulling her to him, his mouth brushed hers. His kiss was brief, but that didn't lessen its impact. Stunned, Harri's cheeks colored under the heat of his gaze.

"We wouldn't want to disappoint Magnolia," he explained.

"No . . . we wouldn't."

"You let Mike kiss you often?" His gaze traveled with tantalizing expertise over her pink mouth.

"No . . . not often." Harri was encouraged that it was a more than casual interest she heard in his tone.

"Kissing the help just because they do their jobs sounds a little more than friendly."

Their eyes met and refused to give in. "Well, you know Mike."

"I do know Mike. That's what concerns me."

She smiled. "I'll bet you don't lose any sleep over it. I'm late for work, have to run."

Leaning against the doorway, he watched as she carried Magnolia back across the lawn. He wasn't going to lose any sleep over Mike, but the kiss—he wasn't so sure.

Why did you kiss her, Malone? And don't try and tell me it was because the monkey wanted you to.

No, she was getting to him, and he wasn't sure how he felt about it.

He suddenly straightened, calling to her. "Don't forget the ice cream!"

"I won't," she called back.

As she disappeared into her house, he turned and walked back into the kitchen.

Whistling, he walked past the hall mirror, catching a brief glimpse of himself as he passed.

Walking on, he suddenly stopped and backed up, groaning aloud when he saw the way his hair was standing straight up on end.

Shaking his head, he started to grin at the comical image.

Malone, if she actually lets you buy her an ice cream cone after seeing you looking like this, you'd better come clean with her. She's one in a million.

Five

Late Sunday afternoon a puff of white smoke came through Shae's office window.

A few moments later, another one, then another one.

Shae knew if he were at the Vatican, it would have meant a new Pope had been elected. But since he was sitting in his office in Cloverdale, he was reasonably sure that it was only Harri cooking out again.

Sighing, he stood up and went to close the window. If he'd just give in and turn on the air conditioner, her activities wouldn't distract him as easily, but he felt confined with the windows closed.

He was about to close the window anyway when he noticed a man coming out of Harri's back door.

Leaning closer to the windowpane, he felt a spark of jealousy when he recognized Mike Stevenson. Though it had been years since he had seen him, Mike hadn't changed that much. He was still tall, blond, arrogant, and easily able to attract women.

Harri's laughter drifted up to him, and Shae leaned closer to see what was so funny.

Ignore her, Malone, he told himself. She had a right to her personal life.

Still, the thought of her with Mike bothered him. If Mike was anything like the randy adolescent he'd been in the eighth grade, Harri didn't need to be chumming around with him.

But what's it to you if she's running around with a womanizer? She's a big girl now. A widow—with a big lonely bed.

His eyes moved over the simple navy blue dress and heels she wore, and the spark of jealousy ignited into a flame. Apparently, she'd just gotten off work and had brought Mike home with her.

Shae closed the window and stepped into the hall to flip on the air conditioner. Returning to the computer, he forced his mind on work again.

What are they doing now? What will they be doing an hour from now? Two hours from now?

After pressing a key to save the document, he turned the computer off, realizing that work was impossible.

He strode into the kitchen and opened the cabinet, removed the coffee can, dumped its contents into the trash can, then let himself out the back door.

Mike glanced up as Shae stepped over the hedge a few moments later.

"Hey, Malone! Harri said you were back in town!"

"Stevenson? Son of a gun! I didn't know you were over here!" The two men slapped each other on the back cordially, then shook hands.

Shae glanced around innocently. "Harri around?"

Mike's smile widened. "She was here a minute ago."

Shae held the empty coffee can up and shook it. "Ran out of caffeine."

Mike nodded toward the house. "She's in there somewhere. Go on in."

Shae climbed the back steps and entered the kitchen. Harri was no where around, but Myron was.

"Ooooh Eeeee! Here's the bod!"

Frowning back at the bird, Shae walked into the living room. "Harri?"

Hearing no response, he walked back through the kitchen.

Overheard, he heard a soft bump and glanced up, realizing that she must be upstairs. After climbing the carpeted steps, he reached the second floor landing and paused. He could hear her voice as she moved about in the bedroom, softly humming.

Following the sound, he moved to the third bedroom on the right and called softly, "Harri, you got any—"

His voice broke off as she whirled, startled by his unexpected appearance. Dazed, he stared at the vision before him. She had just showered and was getting dressed. The smell of her bath powder—soft and seductive, drifted to him.

Clad in a wisp of a bra and bikini lace panties, she was attempting to fasten black nylons to a cream-colored garter belt.

He noticed that she made no attempt to conceal her state of near nudity. "Hi."

"Hi." Shae knew a gentleman would apologize and

turn away, but his eyes refused to leave the beguiling sight.

"Something I can do for you?"

Again, a gentleman would have overlooked her question, but Shae suddenly realized he wasn't one.

Leaning negligently against the doorway, he let his gaze wander over her improperly. "What are you offering?"

She lifted her leg to a small stool, and ran her hand over the stocking to smooth it. "What are you wanting?"

Their eyes met again leisurely.

He held up the empty coffee can. "I'm empty."

"Oh?" She smiled innocently. "Can I help?"

She was teasing him. Shae knew it, but he found the provocative play arousing. He could feel every part of his body responding to the tantalizing display of curves, hollows, and warm, womanly flesh. It wasn't hard for him to see why Patrick had chosen her over all the women in Cloverdale. She was exquisite.

Smiling, she fastened the last nylon, then straightened, giving his eyes another few moments to drink their fill. Mercifully, she finally reached for her robe, and slipped into it, then seated herself at her dressing table. "There's a new can in the pantry. Help yourself."

"I'm not sure I can find it by myself."

Her eyes lifted and met his intimately. "You're a big boy, aren't you?"

Though he didn't answer verbally, his eyes spoke for him.

Turning back to the mirror, she picked up a brush

and pulled it through her hair. "If you can't find it, Mike knows where it is."

She was dismissing him; the game was over. For the first time, Shae didn't want it to be.

But she left him little choice other than to back slowly out of her room, and go in search of the coffee.

Mike glanced up from tending the fire as Shae stepped out of the house a few minutes later. "Find her?"

Clearing his throat, Shae smiled. "Yeah . . . I found her."

"Have you had dinner yet?"

Glancing up at Harri's bedroom window, he returned absently, "No, I had my mind elsewhere."

Mike looked at him puzzled, but merely said, "Well, pull up a chair. We have plenty."

"Thanks, but I don't want to intrude on your evening."

"Harri and I didn't have anything special planned," Mike said. "Besides, I've been meaning to call you."

"Oh?"

"Yeah." Mike grinned. "I want to hit you up for a favor."

The favor turned out to be a plea for Shae to attend the picnic the following Saturday. The zoo was in desperate need of volunteers to help with the turtle and camel rides.

Shae glanced up as Harri came out of the house a few minutes later. A vein in his neck began to pound as she walked toward him wearing a simple, lemon-colored sundress. The dress was backless, strapless, and heartless enough to fell the strongest of men.

"Hey . . . here's the lady now. I'm trying to talk

Shae into giving us a hand with the rides on Saturday," Mike confessed as Harri joined the two men.

Harri's eyes met Shae's serenely. "Have you decided to come?"

"Sorry. I can't spare the time."

"Three hours—four, tops," Mike pleaded. "I'm desperate, Malone. Think of it as your civic duty."

Shae considered Harri a moment longer, then said impulsively, "All right. I guess I can spare an hour or two."

"Terrific! Oh, I asked Shae to join us for dinner," Mike said as Harri moved to stir the coals in the grill.

Her brows lifted. "Oh, can you stay?" she asked, deliberately keeping her tone indifferent.

"Sure, why not."

If you think I'm going to walk away and leave you alone with Stevenson when I know what you're wearing beneath that dress, forget it.

"Sure, why not," she returned lightly. Turning, she smiled. "I'll get you a glass of lemonade." Brushing past him, she murmured, "I know you must be warm."

"Hey!" The next morning Shae placed his index and middle fingers to his mouth, and whistled shrilly. "You want to hold it down out there?"

After a sleepless night, he had finally rolled out of bed before dawn, and had been working steadily for the past five hours. But suddenly there was a racket going on below his window.

From his vantage point, he could see a crowd gathering on the walk in front of Harri's house.

Women and small children milled around on the sidewalk as a small group of elderly men wearing V.F.W. Post hats unpacked brass musical instruments from black leather cases.

Shae viewed the scene with growing apprehension. The crowd, comprised mostly of women, appeared to be restless and on edge.

Relieved, Shae spotted Harri coming around the corner of her house carrying a placard with the statement LIVE AND LET LIVE in bold black lettering.

He leaned out the window and whistled again.

Glancing up, she sent him a friendly wave. "Good morning!"

"What's going on?"

"Didn't I tell you?"

"Tell me what?"

"We're just having a demonstration! It'll be over in a jiffy!"

"A demonstration!" Shae's eyes distraughtly surveyed the crowd that had swelled to close to thirty-five people. He guessed it would be considered a crowd in Cloverdale. "About what?"

"About the cypress tree in front of mom's house! The city wants to remove it to install new sewer lines. The tree's been here for over a hundred years, and mom would have a heart attack if I let them cut it down. I've organized a few of the neighbors for a protest!"

The sound of sirens drowned out her voice as two black and white police cars wheeled around the corner, speeding toward the scene of the disturbance.

Dogs barked, babies cried, and toddlers squealed at the top of their lungs as they tried to escape their mothers' hold.

The whole scene put Shae in mind of a three-ring circus. As the commotion grew louder, various posters began to pop up throughout the crowd:

CHAIN SAW MURDERER!

MAYOR BAILEY, WON'T YOU PLEASE GO HOME!

JOHNNY PAYCHECK SAYS TAKE THIS TREE AND SAVE IT!

A patrolman riding a motorcycle flew around the corner with his siren blaring, heralding the arrival of Mayor Bailey's long black limousine.

Shae could see the mayor sitting in the back seat, mopping his brow with a large handkerchief as he viewed the size of the swelling mob.

Harri yelled something up at Shae again, but because of all the confusion, it was impossible for him to hear her.

Waving off whatever she was trying to relay to him, he closed the window to block out the melee.

"Damn madhouse around here," he mumbled as he sat back down at the computer. "Can't get anything done. If it isn't snakes and monkeys, it's a bunch of loonies swarming around with placards."

You have to go to the suburbs, Shae, nothing in Cloverdale but peace and quiet—well, Dad, for two cents I'd pack up and go back to Manhattan. I could set up office in Grand Central Station and get more done.

The phone jangled, severing his concentration again. Disgusted, Shae leaned back in his chair, listening as it rang three times.

The answering machine clicked on, and he heard his voice reciting a monotone message assuring the caller that he'd reached the Malone residence and that if he had enough patience to watch paint dry, he would eventually return the call.

Then Gretchen's voice came on the line, "Shae, I'm getting tired of talking to this machine. This is the third time I've called this week, and you haven't returned one of my calls yet. Are you sick?"

"Very," Shae returned tightly, "of interruptions."

"Fred and Jenny have tickets for the opera Saturday night. Drive into the city early because Jenny has made reservations for us at Pappadores, so don't be late—and don't tell me you have to work! You work too hard as it is, and you need a break. Remember, all work and no play makes Shae a dull boy—oh, and wear your blue suit."

A beep followed and then the sound of the tape rewinding.

Reaching for a pencil, Shae irritably marked Saturday off on his calendar. The last thing he wanted to do was go to the opera, and he'd been taking nothing but breaks from his work from the minute he'd arrived in Cloverdale. He couldn't afford to lose the whole day Saturday driving into the city, but if he didn't go, Gretchen would be disappointed. It was clearly another one of those no-win situations. A loud pounding at his back door was the last straw.

Tossing the pencil straight up into the air, Shae gave up. The gods were against his ever getting to chapter five.

Jerking the door open a few moments later, he found a man sitting on a large cage, mopping his brow with a red and white bandanna. "Delivery for Ms. Whitlock."

"You've got the wrong house. Ms. Whitlock lives next door."

The man wearily dragged himself to his feet, then reached for the clipboard he'd laid on the porch steps. Shae could see the man's name, HANK, embroidered on the front left pocket of his shirt. It was only eleven in the morning, but because of the sweltering humidity, Hank didn't have a dry thread on him.

"Ms. Whitlock says you'll have to accept it for her." The man thrust the clipboard under Shae's nose. "Sign here."

Shae's glanced toward Harri's house resentfully. "Why can't she accept it?"

"Can't get my truck through all those crazies." Hank reached up to mop his forehead again as he peered over the hedge next door.

Shae reached out and scribbled his name across the receipt. "What's going on over there, anyway?"

"Beats me. Something about a tree." Turning, he hefted the large crate up into his arms, looking at Shae expectantly. "Where do you want it, buddy?"

"I don't know—just set it down here in the kitchen, I guess."

The man wobbled through the doorway, trying to distribute the weight of the large damaged box evenly on his small frame.

"You need some help with that?" Shae offered.

"Nope." A moment later, Hank banged the crate down on the floor, then fumbled for his handkerchief again. "It's murder out there today."

Shae nodded, eyeing the box that had COLOMBIA stamped on both sides along with multiple warnings to HANDLE WITH CARE and KEEP IN AN UPRIGHT POSITION. What in the hell was this?

"What's in there?" Shae asked.

The delivery man looked at the box. "Damned if I know. Picked it up at the airport about an hour ago." Giving his forehead one last swipe, the man turned to leave, then added, "Whatever it is, she's tough to balance."

Shae believed him. The box was beaten completely out of shape.

He turned to open the refrigerator to take out a cola. As he lifted the drink to his mouth, he felt something fly by his shoulder. Lifting his gaze slowly, he found a small, strange-looking bird perched on the light fixture above his head.

Stunned, he realized what the package was. "What the—?"

Suddenly, his eyes widened as the room came alive with a horrible screech and a panic of flapping wings. The bird flew by his face again.

He reeled backward, his drink went flying across the floor as he ducked to dodge the pounding wings and flying feathers. The bird, confused by his new surroundings, was frenzied as it made a frantic bid for its freedom. Shae was beginning to like some of Harri's animals, but birds gave him the creeps.

Shielding his head, Shae bolted for the open doorway. Bursting from the porch into the yard, he sprinted across the lawn, leaping over the hedges as he came to them. If Harri thought he was going to babysit for a vicious bird while she was out trying to save a tree, she was nuts!

By now, the crowd of concerned citizens gathered to save the cypress tree had swelled to an angry mob.

The V.F.W. ensemble was tooting out a rousing—

though slightly off-key—version of "When the Saints Come Marching In."

Young women with moussed hair and faces flushed by heat milled about, waving their placards, trying to outshout each other.

Uniformed police were standing by in case of trouble, their hands folded behind their backs, their faces fixed in the same indifferent mask. The thermometer hovered at a scorching ninety-five degrees, making the situation feel even more volatile.

The mayor had climbed onto the tailgate of a pickup in an attempt to explain to the angry mob why the tree must be cut to install new sewer lines.

A harried young mother in the crowd, who was struggling to control three cranky toddlers, who were two hours overdue for their naps, angrily cast loud aspersions on the mayor's mother and grandmother.

Tempers were flaring as Shae elbowed his way though the crowd trying to find Harri. He had no intention of becoming involved in this madhouse; all he wanted was to find Harri and demand that she remove the bird from his kitchen immediately.

Just as a small fracas broke out around the tailgate the mayor was perched upon he finally spotted her.

"Harri!" he shouted.

Harri whirled at the sound of his voice. Her hair was drooping like a limp dishrag and her face was flushed with heat. The placard she was holding showed signs of recent shoe marks where it had been trampled by the crowd. "What?"

"I want to talk to you!"

"Not now!"

The brass ensemble switched to a deafening "Beer

Barrel Polka" as a placard came sailing over Shae's head.

He ducked, and the placard barely missed him as it landed in the flower bed.

"There is a bird flying around in my kitchen!" he shouted as his head came up again.

Harri tried to push her way through the crowd to him. "Why did you open the crate?"

"I didn't! The damn crate was damaged."

"Sorry," she shouted, "I'll be there in a minute."

"Not in a minute—right now!"

"Shae, I can't leave right now!"

The police began wading into the crowd to break up a hair-pulling contest that had suddenly erupted among five of the protesters. Apples and oranges started flying as complete bedlam broke out.

Shae scrambled to prevent Harri from becoming involved. "Let's get out of here," he warned. "The police are starting to make arrests!"

The fracas was growing noisier as Harri began to work her way toward him.

A policeman stepped up to Shae and shouted above the din. "Break it up, buddy."

"Now look here," Shae snapped. "I'm not part of this—"

"I said move it, buddy, before I run you in for disturbing the peace."

With his eyes on Harri, Shae raised his palm to halt the officer. "Hold on a minute," he ordered, but before he could say another word, the officer grabbed his wrists and pulled him off balance, then jerked Shae's hands behind his back to snap the cuffs in place.

"Listen, officer, I'm not this—I was only—"

"Save it for the judge, buddy."

The officer began to hustle Shae through the chaotic crowd. Harri's eyes widened in disbelief, and she began shoving her way through a maze of bodies, calling to the officer who had Shae by the arm. "Wait a minute! He didn't do anything," she shouted.

"Move it, lady."

"This isn't fair—he isn't involved in this! If you're going to arrest someone, it ought to be me!"

"Harri, stay out of this," Shae warned, shooting her an apprehensive glance. "Just take care of that damn bird!"

"But Shae, I organized this rally," she began in a logical tone, "if these fools are going to make arrests, it should be the people responsible, not an innocent bystander like you!"

"Well, that can be arranged, lady."

With that, a second officer drew Harri's hands behind her back and cuffed her.

Well, Harri thought, at least it was more fair now.

"You know what our problem was?" Harri asked.

The cell doors slid open, and Shae stepped out. "No exactly what was *our* problem?" he returned calmly.

Harri's footsteps matched his as they echoed down the jail corridor.

"I didn't have the demonstration as well organized as I should have," she admitted. "Maybe next time we could—"

"Lady," Shae said evenly, "if it weren't for the fact that I've just spent the last six hours sitting in a jail cell that I don't ever want to see again, your life wouldn't be worth a plug nickle." He had been right about Harri all along; she was still making his life a misery.

Harri paused, and her eyebrows lifted. "Well!"

Nodding gravely, Shae accepted the envelope containing his personal effects from the desk sergeant.

A moment later, Harri and Shae stepped out of the police station into the bright sunshine.

"I know you're upset about this, and you have every right to be," she said. "After all, you've lost another day's work—well, no, I guess that's two days work—"

Shae slowed, his eyes turning to her incredulously. "*Two* days?"

"Well . . . tomorrow is Saturday."

"So?"

"So, you promised Mike you'd be at the picnic to help with the rides."

Shae started to walk again. "I've changed my mind."

"You can't change your mind. If it weren't for Mike, we'd still be sitting on those lumpy mattresses," she reminded. "He was the one who posted our bail."

"Harri, I'd rather be strapped buck naked to the town clock than lose another day on this book!"

"Nevertheless, you promised to give us a hand."

"I can't go," Shae argued. "I'm behind forty pages on the book this week because of all these confounded interruptions." Gretchen's earlier message suddenly came back to him, causing him to add curtly, "Besides, I have to take Gretchen to the opera tomorrow night."

Harri paused, looking as stunned as if Shae had slapped her face. "Gretchen?" she asked softly.

"Yes . . . Gretchen . . . and get that look off your face!"

"What look?" She tried, but she couldn't hide her disappointment.

"Like I just shot your dog."

"Who's Gretchen?" Her tone was not as nonchalant as she'd hoped.

They started walking again, their eyes searching for Harri's Volkswagen.

"Where did Mike say he left the car?"

"He said it was on the front row closest to the street."

Harri knew that Shae wasn't a monk, so why should the discovery that he was seeing someone have such a devastating effect on her?

"You could break your date," she blurted.

His pace slowed. "What?"

"You can see your girlfriend anytime; our fund-raiser comes only once a year."

Shae shifted restlessly. The rays of the sinking sun caught his hair, turning it a fiery red.

Harri was positive that he had never looked more appealing. There was no longer any doubt in her mind. She was still in love with him. Hopelessly, incurably, in love. And she was certain that she was further from winning his love now than she had been fifteen years ago.

"Break a date? I can't do that to Gretchen."

Turning, Harri started away. She would not allow him see the moisture gathering in her eyes. He'd made his choice, she wouldn't beg. Had she really expected him to keep a commitment to her?

Yes, fool that she was, that's exactly what she'd

expected. He'd agreed to help at the fund-raiser; she'd thought he was a man of his word.

"Where are you going?" he demanded.

She didn't respond. She couldn't have answered him if she'd wanted to because of the painful lump that was suddenly crowding her throat.

"Answer me!"

Harri kept walking, her feet moving over the pavement faster.

"Well if this isn't a fine mess," she heard him mutter. "Is this a jealous snit, Harriet—is that what this is all about?" He shifted his stance irritably. "I didn't say I planned to father Gretchen's children. I only mentioned that I was going to take her to the opera—come back here!" he demanded as she slipped behind the wheel of her car still refusing to look at him.

"Well," he challenged, "just how long did good ole Mike hang around after I left last night?" He had to leap out of the way as Harri floored her Volkswagen and roared past him.

He watched, hands on his hips, engulfed by a cloud of blue exhaust.

"Okay, so I'll go to the damn picnic," he conceded lamely.

A moment later, he trudged off in the direction of home, wondering what he'd done to deserve such misery.

Six

"You like mustard or ketchup on your hot dog?"

Shae glanced up late Saturday afternoon, relieved to find Harri standing on the sidelines holding two paper plates.

In the past hour, a five hundred pound turtle had stepped on his foot, and the camel had spit on him twice.

"At this point, I'd eat it with grape jelly," he confessed.

Harri caught Mike's eye and lifted the two plates hopefully. "Do you care if I steal your help for awhile?"

"It's my turn ta ride the elphant, mister!" a small boy reminded impatiently as he tugged at Mike's shirt tail.

Mike hefted the boy into the saddle to join four other sweaty munchkins. "Fifteen minutes, Harri! Not a minute longer."

Shae followed Harri to a large oak where an old army blanket was spread and waiting. Dropping onto the ground, he reached for the paper cup she was filling with lemonade from a red thermos. "I'm so dry I could spit cotton," he admitted.

Harri finished filling the two cups, then dropped down on the blanket beside him. "The response has been wonderful," she remarked. "The proceeds from the picnic should provide more than enough funds to build a new aviary."

They sat silently for a moment, enjoying the hint of breeze rustling through the treetops. The day was warm and muggy, typical of late June.

"This is nice. I have to hand it to Mike; he's got a first class operation here."

"He's worked very hard," Harri admitted. "Since he was named director, he has opened exhibits for the bald eagle, the bull elephant, the black panther, and four species of lemur—a relative of a monkey. Cloverdale should be proud of Mike's accomplishments."

Shae lay back to stretch out on the blanket. A fly droned lazily around his head as his eyes drifted shut.

"Shae?"

"Hmm?"

"What made you change your mind about coming today?"

Harri had been astonished when she'd come out of her house this morning and found him waiting on the back steps.

"Did I have a choice?" he returned dryly.

"Of course you had a choice."

He didn't fool her. He was having more fun than he'd admit. During the drive to the picnic grounds, he had complained about wasting another whole day, but each time that she'd checked to see how he was doing, he was having a good time.

Harri had to admit that no matter how obstinate he could be, she enjoyed his company. When they were together, she felt comfortable enough to kick off her shoes and shake out her hair, and she didn't give a second thought to her lipstick having disappeared hours ago. She had to admit she liked the feeling it gave her. She had yet to experience the same kind of contentment with any other man.

"What kind of a marriage did you and Patrick have?"

Startled, Harri wondered if Shae had read her mind. "Patrick was very good to me," she said carefully.

"Most people are 'very good' to their dogs," Shae returned in a drowsy voice. "Were you in love with him?"

Wrapping her arms around her knees, she gazed at the sky, thinking about those restless years. "Maybe at first, but Patrick was gone so much. His career took precedence after a few months, and I came in a distant second."

Shae studied her from beneath lowered lashes. "Would you still be in love with him if Patrick were alive?"

"I don't know . . . That question haunted me for a long time after his death. Now, I guess it's irrelevant. Patrick's gone, leaving me a smarter woman."

"How?"

"Well for one thing, a woman shouldn't marry a man because he has wide shoulders and looks terrific in a football jersey."

Grinning, Shae sat up and reached for one of the

paper plates. Taking a bite out of the hot dog, he winked at her. "So what are the right ingredients for a good marriage?"

Stealing a chip from his plate, she winked back at him. "I don't know. I haven't had a good one yet."

The food on their plates dwindled as the subject was abandoned in favor of a more palatable diversion.

"What did Gretchen say?"

"About what?"

"About your coming to the picnic."

"She was disappointed, but she understood."

Why was she hoping to hear that the mysterious Gretchen had been less genial, Harri wondered, then she was instantly ashamed of her thoughts.

"Why did you change your mind?" she asked softly, avoiding eye contact.

"I don't know. . . . Do you think it's possible I wanted to spend the day with you more?" He winked at her again.

"I guess anything is possible."

For a long moment, they looked at each other. Nothing more needed to be said. Both were aware of the slim, but binding thread beginning to form between them. For no other reason than she wanted to, Harri reached over and laced her fingers with his.

"Thank you."

"No, thank you." His eyes met hers. "I'd forgotten what it was like to relax."

Squeezing each other's hand, they lay back, gazing into a stunning, azure blue sky.

"Shae?"

"Hmm?"

"Why haven't you married yet?"

He was so quiet that she thought at first he hadn't heard her. Then he answered quietly, "I'm not sure . . . the time never seemed right, or the woman."

"Did you ever come close?"

"Once, a long time ago."

"Tell me about her."

"We were in our sophomore year of college. We'd been dating for several months, and Kristen suddenly decided she wanted to elope." Shae smiled, realizing he hadn't thought about Kristen or that night in years. The idea had popped up at a New Year's Eve party they had been attending . . . too much beer, too much unbridled lust.

"We looked up a Justice of the Peace and got him out of bed in the middle of the night. The old man and his wife agreed to perform the ceremony. Just as I was about to say 'I do' I realized 'I didn't.' "

Harri smiled, picturing a young Shae standing in front of a minister, about to take a bride. "You didn't what?"

"I didn't want to be responsible for another life. Kristen and I weren't in love—at least, not enough to commit to a lifetime together. I couldn't do that to her, or to me, so I called it off at the last minute."

"Was she upset?"

"I don't know—she giggled about it for days, and three weeks later she dumped me for a guard on the basketball team. What do you think?"

Smiling, she gazed up at the sky, remembering the day she and Patrick were married. At the last minute, she had been tempted to run, but one look at her parents' beaming faces, and she'd known she'd had to see it through. At times she had wished she had listened to her heart.

"You must have been in love with Patrick, or you wouldn't have married him," Shae said quietly, finding that the revelation disturbed him.

Harri sighed. "I guess I was—or thought I was at the time. Isn't that why most people marry?"

"No, sometimes people marry for all the wrong reasons."

"Well, Patrick loved me in his own way, but he was trying to make a name for himself. He was gone constantly after the first year. He started buying lavish gifts and sending them to me in an effort to make up for his absence. For a long time I believed the gifts were an expression of his love and that they were his way of trying to make our marriage work. But when he died, I discovered that he had been involved with one of the groupies who followed athletes, so I can only assume that he sent all those lovely gifts out of guilt."

Shae propped his head on his elbow, studying her. "I'm sorry. I didn't mean to stir up painful memories."

"No, it's all right. I've accepted what Patrick did a long time ago."

"And you're not bitter about it?"

"I accepted it; I didn't say I liked it."

"Then you don't rule out getting married again?"

"No. I plan to."

She dated occasionally. There was Mike—and Phil, a bank vice-president, Bryon, a stock broker. But she felt no electricity with them, no giddy, I-can't-live-without-you feeling that she was determined to find this time.

She knew the emotion existed—her friends had talked about it too often for her to believe that that kind of love could only be found in books and movies, but the closest she'd come to having such a feeling was when Magnolia had forced Shae to give her that innocuous brush across her mouth. And that didn't count.

She didn't have to read his lips to know that he considered her a notch more annoying than a common cold sore.

"I'm happy with my life the way it is."

"Maybe it's because you can't get a man to look at you, huh, Harriet?" Lying back again, he watched to see if she was taking the ribbing with her usual savoir-faire. When he saw that she was, he relaxed.

"Maybe you're tired of living, huh, Shae?" Sitting up, she reached for her cup, empty now except for the melting ice.

Tipping the cup forward, she let a stream of icy water trickle down the front of his shirt.

Without opening his eyes, his hands came out to capture hers. "Women have died for less than that," he said calmly.

She laughed, trying to free herself from his hold.

Rolling to his side, he pinned her to the ground. They struggled, rolling around on the blanket as she pitted her strength against his. She was considerably overpowered and knew it. "Shae, stop it! We're attracting attention," she said breathlessly.

Fumbling for his cup, he held her firmly in place as his fingers retrieved an ice cube, then he shoved it down the front of her dress. He laughed when she protested indignantly. "What's the matter, Harriet? Can't take your own medicine?" he teased.

"Shae!"

"Okay," he relented. "I'll take it out." His hand

started after the ice cube as hers shot out to block his effort.

"Hold it."

He grinned. "Why not? I can remember a time when you wouldn't have stopped me."

"There was a time when I didn't have anything down there BUT an ice cube."

Her struggling ceased as his gaze began a leisurely inspection over the front of her blouse. "And you're telling me you do now?"

Her gaze met his smugly. "What do you think?"

The grin he flashed her was the old, mischievous Shae she remembered so well. "That you would slap my face if I told you what I was thinking."

"Not necessarily."

His eyes traveled over her with a faint glow of amusement. The game was on again. "You're pretty sure of yourself, aren't you?"

She gazed back at him, aware of his hand resting lightly on the side of her breast. The contact was casual, but no less provocative.

"Not as sure as I would like to be."

His fingers closed around her breast, causing a wave of pleasure to wash over her. "Admit it, Malone, you've finally found *something* about Harriet Whitlock that interests you."

An easy smile played at the corners of his mouth. "Well, I will admit you've turned out to be a damn good-looking woman," he conceded.

Her pulse quickened as he moved her closer.

"I assume since I've 'turned out' to be such a good-looking woman you won't sleep again until you've tasted the sweetness of my lips?"

"No, I don't think I'll have any trouble sleeping."

"Ah, but should you take such a chance. Now that it has suddenly dawned on you that I, Harriet—"

"By the way," he interrupted. "Who's idea was it to name you Harriet?"

Harri winced. "My mother. She named me after her favorite sister. My Aunt Harriet? You remember when we were in the seventh grade, and I wore those horrible skirts and knitted vests to school every day?"

Shae nodded. The memory was permanently etched in his mind.

Harriet following him down the hallways, *calling to him* in front of the other boys, wearing her hair in those silly little clumps that *bobbled* on each side of her head as she walked.

The humiliation was more than any thirteen-year-old should be forced to endure.

"They were Aunt Harriet's handiwork," Harri confessed. "I cried every morning when I had to put them on, but mother insisted I wear them for fear I'd hurt Aunt Harriet's feelings."

She could feel the heat of his body coursing through hers, and it set off an aching response. For all the bad things about her marriage, Patrick had been a consummate lover; for that reason it had been even harder for her to adjust to his death.

Gazing into Shae's eyes right now, she wondered if he could see her hunger.

"What would you do if I kissed you?" she whispered.

His mouth curved into an unconscious smile. "I don't know."

Her arms lifted to encircle his neck gently. "Well, if the idea disturbs you, think of it this way. You're a man and I'm a woman—"

"Yeah, I about had that figured out." His hand became openly bolder and she knew she should stop him, but she didn't.

"When Kim Novak took William Holden on a picnic, she didn't have to beg him to kiss her," she reminded.

"Now you're Kim Novak?"

"It's possible—for instance, if I met a man like you who had long, reddish-gold eyelashes and incredibly blue eyes, why, it's possible I could even bypass Kim Novak and move right on to say—Kim Basinger?"

"Kim Basinger?" His eyes moved over her mouth with a lazy assuredness. "The devil you say."

Slowly drawing his mouth closer, she realized that she had never been so brazen, not even with Patrick. "How about it, Malone, want to test the theory?"

Their mouths brushed, and she felt her stomach knot with desire.

"Uh-uh."

"Uh-uh?" Her brow lifted. "Why not?" she whispered. He could not use the excuse that he didn't want her. He did. She could feel the incriminating evidence pressing against her thigh.

"Because there's a man and woman coming toward us who look like they are seriously considering turning a hose on us," he whispered back, brushing his mouth across hers a second time.

White-hot fire raced through her as their mouths came back together again, this time with more urgency.

It took a moment for his warning to penetrate her muddled senses. When it did, she hurriedly bolted upright, brushing the remnants of leaves from her hair. He had completely made her forget where they were.

Sneaking a sheepish look in the direction of the animal rides, she was relieved to find Mike still absorbed with the children.

Shae chuckled and lay back on the blanket as the elderly couple walked past them. "Are you afraid your boss will see us?"

"No, of course not," she murmured.

"What's with the two of you?"

She noticed his tone was more insistent than it had been in the past when they had spoken about Mike. Leaning closer, she whispered, "We're madly in love, but we don't want anyone to know it—especially you."

He shot her an annoyed look. He didn't know why, but Mike was beginning to irritate him.

The man was obviously interested in Harri. That was understandable. She was a good-looking woman. Shae would even admit to himself that for a crazy moment, he had even desired her—no, wanted her. He wanted her. More than wanted her—he was getting involved with her. This was no longer a game. He was beginning to fall in love with her, even though he knew he should back off.

"A penny for your thoughts?"

"You'd be overcharged," he responded evasively.

"The book again?"

"I'm always thinking about the book," he admitted.

Laying her hand on his arm, she asked softly, "Can I help?"

"No." Rolling to his side, he shoved aside the urge to take her in his arms again.

"Tell me where you are in the plot."

Sighing, Shae told her the story thus far.

"That's good . . . really good," she mused. "But why not have the poor old *grandmother* be the murderer."

"She's blind," he reminded.

"Maybe, maybe not." Sitting up, Harri mulled the plot over in her mind. "Perry Beal would lead his reader to believe that the woman is blind when she really wasn't." Warming to the idea, her eyes sparkled with excitement. "No, she's not blind at all; she's been lying to the heroine all these years!"

Shae smiled, amazed at the way her thoughts meshed so well with his. "Or the sister-in-law committed the crime."

Harri turned, her face filling with awe. "Of course, Shae—why that's brilliant! Everyone thinks the sister-in-law is in an irreversible coma!"

Shae grinned as she reached over and hugged him tightly. Catching her to him, he hugged her back.

"You're wonderful," she praised. "Monday, I'll stop by the book store and buy every one of Perry Beal's novels for you—"

"Harri," he cut in uneasily.

"No, I know what you're going to say. 'You can't afford it.' Well, forget it. I was saving to buy myself a new coat, but the books are more important. Study Beal's work. With a little practice, you're capable of being as good or better." She stilled his protest again. "My old coat is still perfectly serviceable, I'm just tired of it."

Shae felt like the world's prize heel. "Harri, look, there's something you should know about me—"

She stopped him again. "Really, Shae, I don't mind.

You couldn't have a better teacher—Beal is a master at plotting, but Jack Mitcheson is better if you having trouble with dialogue." She looked thoughtful. "I'll pick up a couple of his novels too."

Shae glanced at her accusingly. "There's nothing wrong with Beal's dialogue."

Harri wrinkled her nose. "Well . . . Mitcheson is better."

They glanced up at the sound of Mike's voice calling frantically for help. Harri stood up and waved, signaling that they were coming.

"Guess we've overstayed our limit." Extending her hand, Shae took it, getting to his feet.

Their gazes met, and she smiled. "Shae, I know how important it is to you to be published, and you will. Just be patient." She paused, seeing the indecision in his eyes. "I want to help—no strings attached, honest." She crossed her heart.

The love in her eyes made him decide to end the ruse, here and now.

"Harri, I am Perry Beal," he confessed, wondering if she would ever speak to him again.

Lifting her hands she smoothed his beard, something undefinable lighting her eyes now. "You bet you are," she whispered softly. "And one of these days you'll find a publisher who'll recognize the similarity."

"No, Harri—listen to me. I am—"

"Malone, help!" Mike shouted.

"Shhh, kiss me once more," she murmured.

Issuing a low groan, he felt her curves nestle against him as his hold tightened around her waist. Lifting her in the cradle of his arms, he kissed her hungrily, turning her in a slow, lazy circle.

Closing her eyes, she rejoiced in the feel of his maleness stirring against her. He was not immune to her.

Not any more.

For as long as she could remember, she had been in love with this man. Was it any wonder that the soft contours of her body were shamelessly welcoming every inch of him pressed tightly against her?

His scent intoxicated her, made her light-headed, made her wish that they were anywhere but in a crowded park with hundreds of other people looking on.

He rocked her back and forth, their mouths fused tightly. She had lived this moment in her fantasies a hundred—no, a million or more times.

Shae Malone was kissing her—and something even more miraculous—he was enjoying it.

Mike shouted again, causing Shae to reluctantly lower her back to her feet, his hands easing gently over the flare of her hips. He stared down at her, his hands still cupping her buttocks lightly.

"We need to talk, Harri."

She took satisfaction in the knowledge that his voice wasn't as steady as it had been earlier. "About what?"

His eyes moved over her nubile curves, painfully aware of how much he needed her. "About a lot of things."

Pulling his mouth back to hers, she murmured, "You say when." As far as she was concerned, they had the rest of their lives.

Seven

Five copies of Perry Beal's books and two of Mitcheson's were propped next to Shae's bottle of milk on the front porch the next morning. Feeling like an award-winning jerk, he picked them up and read the brief note attached to Harri's presents. "Here's the best. Study them." The phone was ringing when Shae walked back into the house again. Picking up the ringing extension in the kitchen, he knew the caller would be his father before he answered. Jess Malone had called twice the evening before.

"I'm sorry, Dad, but it's just not possible."

"Well hello to you too," his father answered. "Listen, Shae, work with them on this. They've moved the book up a couple of months because the public is crying for it."

"Dad, I don't see how I can do it," Shae argued. "I'm only half-way through the book. It's impossible to finish it two months early."

After Shae heard Jess's message that Lila was

pushing to have the book completed two months ahead of schedule, he hadn't slept a wink. He was not Superman.

"Why not? What are you doing with all your time?" Jess demanded.

Sighing, Shae moved to stare out the picture window, wondering if he should even try to explain the python, the monkey, the crated Colombian bird, the afternoon in jail, the picnic, the camel with a spitting problem, the ill-mannered, five-hundred-pound turtle, and Harri . . . No, even he found them all hard to believe. "It would be a hundred page chapter, Dad."

"What do you mean, a 'hundred page chapter'? What's that supposed to mean?"

"Let's drop it. I'm going to need the full amount of time on this book."

Perching on the side of his desk, Shae thought about how everything in his life was suddenly taking a backseat to Harri, including his work. He had always been so driven before.

But Harriet just wasn't the same Harriet any more. Every time he saw a sexy woman lately he found himself thinking, *Harri's sexier.* Just last week he'd planned to drive into the city to take Gretchen to dinner, but when his Corvette had failed to start, he'd ended up helping Harri weed a flower bed and had had a better time.

And right now, as he was talking to his *father,* no less, he was watching Harri water her mother's potted geraniums and was becoming aroused.

What had happened to his nice, sane life?

"Well, you'd better find out what you do with your time," Jess was saying.

"Dad, I'm not a twenty-year-old any more, and I'm doing the best I can." Jess lost sight of that occasionally.

"Lila thinks you have too many old friends in Cloverdale, and that's why you haven't been able to turn your chapters in. She thinks you should go into complete seclusion for the next few weeks and at least be in the position to hand in a rough draft by the middle of next month."

Shae's eyes followed Harri as she walked to her car. "Is my editor offering to pay the bill on this little brainstorm?"

"You bet your sweet tush she is. Lila says the boys at the top have said there'll be an extra ten thousand if you can deliver on time."

Shae thought about it. Ten thousand extra for delivering the book eight weeks early? It was tempting.

But was it tempting enough for him to drop out of sight for the next few weeks? His gaze moved back to Harri. He wasn't sure. Perhaps he preferred to spend time with her.

"Lila's set up everything. You'll be getting an express package any minute with hotel accommodations and spending money."

"What about air fare?"

"You won't need it. You can drive to where you're going."

"I don't like it, Dad. I hate to work under this kind of pressure."

"Are you having trouble with the plot?"

No, thanks to Harri, the book was destined to be his best.

"No, there isn't any problem, I just don't want to spit my books out like some robot."

"You don't. You're good, damn good. Drop out of sight for few weeks and see what you come up with."

When Shae hung up, he realized that the conversation had put him in a foul mood. For the first time in his writing career, the pressure was getting to him.

The bad mood stayed with him all day, and by evening he found that his impatience had leapt beyond his control when he saw the smoke from Harri's grill coming into his window again.

Raising the screen, he rested his arms on the sill. "Oh, Harrieeeeettt," he called.

Harri glanced up at the sound of his voice. "Yessssss?" she called back.

"What are you doingggg?"

"I'm starting a firrrrre!"

"Well, knock it offfff. The smoke is drifting into my windowwww."

"Then I suggest you shut your windowwww."

Harri winced as she heard the window bang shut a moment later. Chancing a quick glance in his direction, she saw him jerking the curtain back in place.

Returning to her kitchen, she paused before the hall mirror to take a look at herself. A long, sensible look.

"Harri Whitlock, you're the world's biggest fool," she muttered, admonishing the almost pathetic-looking image staring back at her.

"When are you ever going to get it through your thick skull that you are never going to snag Shae Malone?"

Snag him?

Ha! Face it Harri. He didn't even like her most of the time.

Okay. She thought she was finally getting somewhere with him the day of the picnic, but what had happened since? Nothing. She lived right next door to the man, and she'd barely seen him the past week. Did that sound like a man in love?

"More orange, please."

Sighing, Harri turned away, disgusted by the moron in the mirror. "Okay, Myron. More orange."

Walking to the refrigerator, she removed the slice of fruit from the crisper, and poked it through the bars of the bird's cage.

While Myron ate, Harri busied herself slicing tomatoes and cleaning lettuce. Mike was expected soon, and she wasn't ready for him. She almost regretted asking him over tonight.

Right now she would like nothing better than to take a cool shower, curl up with a good mystery, and immerse herself in a full-blown case of self-pity.

She hated having these run-ins with Shae. She could not see why it was so hard for them to get along with each other. They were both adults. She no longer ran after him like he was an endangered species—or not that he could tell. Or was it just her?

What if she had been a sophisticated blond who didn't have to pursue him?

Why couldn't *he* pursue her for a change?

And what had happened to that talk he'd said they should have? He hadn't mentioned it again.

Myron's orange suddenly plummeted to the bottom of his cage, and he began hopping around on his perch excitedly. His eyes grew bright with excite-

ment as he strained to see between the bars of his
cage, out the open window. "What a bod! What a
bod!"

"Thanks, Myron," Harri returned absently. "If only
you could convince a certain party living next door
that—"

"WHAT a bod! WooEEEE! Oooh la laaa!" The bird
had gone crazy.

Harri whirled, her knife clattering nosily to the
sink. By now, Myron was hopping back and forth,
unable to conceal his eagerness.

Leaning over to peer out the window, Harri saw
the striking blond walking up Shae's drive.

"Oh, no." Leaning closer to Myron's cage, Harri
whispered reverently, "Who's that?"

The statuesque beauty stepped up on Shae's back
porch and knocked. A moment later, Shae answered
and welcomed her into the house.

Heartsick, Harri straightened. Her spirits were completely dampened. Jealousy, as unwarranted as it
was, threatened to ruin her evening. Glancing helplessly at Myron, she longed to tell someone how she
felt, yet was helpless to explain it, even to herself.

Shae wasn't hers—he would never be. Though she
accepted that, it didn't lessen the hurt of seeing him
with another woman.

She had been living in a dream world the past few
weeks, a wonderful, secure world where Shae locked
himself in his house and worked on his book.

As she turned back to the sink Mike's car pulled
into her drive and she realized that she had to face
reality: Shae was a healthy, attractive man with all
the needs and imperfections of normal, healthy men.
He wasn't a recluse or a hermit, and he was entitled

to a personal life. One that did not, and most likely would not ever, include her.

Biting back tears, she heard Mike rap on the screen door.

"Come in."

"Hi, babe."

"Hi." Wiping the corners of her eyes with a dish towel, Harri turned, wearing her brightest smile. "Hungry?"

"Not too bad, I had a late lunch." He walked across the room to brush a benign kiss across her forehead. "You smell nice."

"Thanks. It's the perfume you gave me last Christmas."

"No kidding." He sniffed her neck again. "I have excellent taste."

Reaching for the hamburger meat, she busied herself by forming individual patties.

"How's the cub?" Mike asked, latching onto a piece of celery from the relish tray.

"Ricky's not too perky today."

Reaching for a glass of lemonade, he trailed behind her as she went out the back door to check the fire.

Harri glanced toward the house next door as she lifted the lid on the grill, wondering what Shae and the blond were doing.

The tall, disgustingly leggy blond.

Surprised, she saw his kitchen curtain drop hastily back into place. Was it possible he was watching her? Her pulse quickened. *Of course not. Grow up, remember, Harri?*

"What do you think about the bids on the monkey house?"

Harri glanced up. "What?"

"The monkey house—what do you think about the bids?" Mike asked, "Too high?"

"Oh—yes. Too high."

A stereo came on, and the voices of Willie Nelson and Julio Iglecias drifted from the house next door.

Harri felt her temper rising. Picking up the bottle of lighter fluid, she gave the coals a liberal dousing again. Slamming the lid back down on the grill, she was determined to ignore Julio's softly accented voice singing, *To alll the girlls I'veee loveed before. . . .*"

Mike stepped out of her way as she brushed past him. "Something wrong?" he called as he watched her march back in the house.

"No." The door slammed behind her a moment later.

She returned in a few minutes to continue their earlier conversation. "How about an annual Halloween Spooktacular for the children? We can expand the FOZ project, and try Adopt-A-Pal again. At Christmas we can decorate with thousands of lights and invite the public to attend for a minimal fee."

"Yeah—that would work." Mike hurriedly stepped aside again as she pushed past him on her way back to the grill. "You sure you don't need any help?"

"No, thanks."

Taking a sip from his glass, he spotted Shae coming out his back door. "Hey, Malone!"

Harri groaned mentally as she heard Shae call back. A moment later, the two men walked toward the hedge. She could hear Mike thanking Shae for helping with the picnic.

It would just be her luck if Mike would invite Shae and his *friend* to eat with them, she fretted. Surely he wouldn't do a thing like that without checking with her first.

But when she stepped out of the house carrying the relish tray a few minutes later, who was sitting on her patio? Shae, the blond, and an openly besotted Mike.

"Guess what?" Mike said brightly.

Harri shot him an anxious look. "You've asked Shae and his guest to join us for dinner."

"Yes! You don't mind, do you?"

YES, she wanted to scream, immensely! *How was she ever going to get over that man if he was continually around?*

"No, I'm happy they could join us," she said.

With considerable effort, Shae managed to catch her attention. "You don't mind?"

She returned a forced smile. "Don't be silly. Of course I don't mind." Was it only her imagination again or was he enjoying her discomfort?

Wearing preppy white shorts and a crisp, yellow sport shirt, he looked so good that it made her teeth ache.

"You're sure now? We wouldn't want to interfere with your evening," he insisted.

She returned his smile, deliberately forcing her eyes away from the crop of thick reddish-gold hair peeping through the opening of his shirt. "I thought you were working tonight."

"I was, but my allergies started acting up." His gaze held hers. "Must be something in the air."

His vague remark referred to the smoke from her grill, and she ignored it. If he didn't like the inconvenience, he could turn on his air conditioner and pay high electric bills just like everyone else.

She shrugged. "Could be."

"Gretchen, I don't believe you've met Harri." Shae reached over to casually drape his arm around the back of Gretchen's chair. "Harri Whitlock, Gretchen Mallory."

Harri's heart sank. *So this was Gretchen. She was gorgeous.*

Harri extended her hand with a warm smile. "I'm so glad you could join us, Gretchen. Shae speaks very highly of you."

Gretchen accepted Harri's hand gratefully. "It's so nice to meet you, Harri. Is there anything I can do to help?"

"No, nothing. Just make yourself comfortable, I'll only be a minute."

Harri disappeared into the house for more hamburger patties and cold drinks. When she returned, she cringed as she realized that Magnolia had slipped out of the house and found herself a perch on the top of Shae's head.

Mike began to laugh, amused by the monkey's antics.

"Hey," Shae shrugged philosophically, "at this point I'm just happy she isn't a water buffalo."

The good-natured remark broke the ice, and to Harri's surprise, the evening went well. Gretchen Mallory turned out to be not only beautiful, but informative and charming. Having worked for a United States Congressman for the past seven years, she had some wildly funny tales about the inner workings of government. Even Shae laughed uproariously a couple of times at her outlandish anecdotes.

Once Harri glanced up to find him watching her.

She grew miserable realizing that he must be comparing her to Gretchen.

But at that moment, Shae was trying to sort through his own confused feelings. When had he stopped comparing her to other women?

His eyes met Harri's and held them again for an uncommonly long time. Harri had to wait until her pulse had settled before she could force herself to break the disturbing eye contact.

"Tell us about you, Harri," Gretchen was saying. "Shae tells me you work with the local zoo, and that you're wonderful with the animals."

Dropping her gaze shyly, Harri began to tell them about her days at the zoo and what her duties were as an assistant director.

Shae watched and listened attentively, interrupting her to add to her list of duties when she happened to leave one out.

It was close to eleven before anyone thought to look at the time. "Eleven o'clock!" Gretchen exclaimed. "I hate to run off like this, but I have over an hour's drive back to the city."

Mike and Shae stood as Gretchen began to gather her personal belongings.

"I have to be going too," Mike admitted. "I have a seven o'clock meeting in the morning with the building committee."

Shae and Gretchen thanked Harri again for the excellent meal, and all four agreed that they would get together again some time soon.

"I thought the meeting with the building committee was scheduled for Monday," Harri remarked as she walked with Mike to his car.

"It is, but Ed Miller's secretary called this afternoon and asked if we could change it to Saturday morning."

As Harri and Mike rounded the corner of the house, Harri hesitated briefly when she noticed that Shae was walking Gretchen to her car.

Deliberately turning her head, she made her mind a blank. She would not watch to see if he kissed her good night. She should be grateful the woman was going home.

She would not look.

But a moment later she was standing on her tiptoes, craning her head over Mike's shoulder, disgusted that she didn't have enough self-respect to spare herself such agony.

Mike turned, glancing over his shoulder. "Something wrong?"

"Oh . . . no . . . you were saying?"

"I was saying that the meeting with the building committee has been changed to tomorrow morning."

"Oh, yes. That's good," she replied, preoccupied by her thoughts.

"And I thought if it was all right with you, I'd sprinkle strychnine on Don Jackson's sweet roll and shoot old Elizabeth Poperight right between the eyes."

"Sure, it's okay with me . . ."

Shae moved Gretchen into the shadows. Harri wondered if he had deliberately blocked her view.

Shaking his head Mike opened the car door. "If you're so crazy about the guy, why don't you do something about it?"

Harri sighed, suddenly aware that she was making a fool out herself. Again. "What's there to do? If I walked up to him naked as a jaybird with my hair on fire, he wouldn't notice."

Mike got into his car and shut the door. "Judging by the way he was looking at you tonight, you underestimate yourself. Take my word for it, kiddo. He'd notice."

Starting the engine, he smiled up at her. "Thanks for the dinner. It was fun."

"Thanks. I enjoyed it too." There were times when Harri desperately wished she was attracted to Mike, and this was one of them. He was a nice, dependable man, overbearing at times, but she knew that she had her faults, too. Unfortunately, the magic just wasn't there.

Gretchen was backing her small sports car out of the drive when Harri turned to go back inside her house.

At least Gretchen and Shae hadn't shared a lengthy, passionate good-bye.

Shae had had barely enough time to walk Gretchen to her car to say good night.

"Need any help cleaning up?"

Harri tensed when she saw Shae walking in her direction again.

"No, thanks."

She started gathering empty cups as he stepped through the opening in the hedge. "Are you sure?"

What was it about him that unfailingly tied her stomach in loops?

Whatever it was, she wished some compassionate scientist would invent a vaccine for it.

"Positive."

"Gretchen said to tell you thanks again. She had a nice time this evening."

"I enjoyed having her."

"Good. We'll do it again some time."

"Sure."

She ignored his devilish grin, and walked over to the trash cart to dump the empty paper plates.

Propping his hip against the picnic table, Shae's grin widened. "I thought you might be interested in taking a look at the book—but, of course, if you're too tired . . ."

The bait was too tempting; that's why he'd thrown it out.

Turning, she looked at him. "You'd let me see your work?"

"Not all of it," he admitted. "I'm superstitious about letting someone read my unfinished work, but I would like your opinion on the chapter that I just finished." He winked at her. "You might recognize certain aspects of the plot."

Her heart began to pound. "I would be honored to read whatever you want me to read."

It only took a few minutes for Shae to retrieve the chapter and return. Handing the stack of papers to her, he poured himself another glass of lemonade as she sat down in the lawn chair and began to read.

She read the twenty-three pages, thoroughly, going back on several occasions to make certain his points were clear, and not confusing to the reader.

When she finished, she lifted her gaze to meet his, her eyes filled with love. "Oh, Shae . . . it's good."

Though she had always known he was talented, she hadn't known until now how unique he was.

His eyes searched hers, almost like a small boy wanting to be assured she just wasn't saying that to please him. "You really think so?"

"I really think so," she said softly.

"I stole your ideas," he confessed.

"Oh, Shae, don't you see? I only have *ideas*. You've been given the gift to breathe life into them."

Reaching for her hand, he squeezed it, overwhelmed by a feeling he was powerless to define. "I could go for a chocolate ice cream cone. How about you?"

"No, thanks." Rising, she handed the papers back to him. He watched as she turned, and started up the steps.

The image of him walking Gretchen to the car, then disappearing behind the bush still tormented her.

"Gretchen and I are not lovers," he said gently.

His admission took Harri by complete surprise. Resting her hand on the screen handle, she listened as he continued.

"Gretchen married my best friend. When the marriage started falling apart at the seams six months ago, she came to me for help. I saw her through a rough time, and she's never forgotten it. There is absolutely nothing between the two of us but a simple friendship."

Warmth flooded Harri's cheeks, and she was ashamed of the way she'd been acting. Shae should not have had to explain that. But she was grateful that he had.

"Okay?" he prompted.

She lifted her eyes and smiled. "Okay."

"Now, how about that ice cream you promised me weeks ago?"

"Sure. I'll get my purse."

It was an almost perfect evening. Overhead, stars twinkled, while a whisper-soft breeze carried the scent of Elinore's roses through the air.

And gardenias. The soft, sultry fragrance engulfed Harri as she came out of her house a moment later.

Shae reached for her hand, and they strolled down a sidewalk drenched in moonlight.

"I did enjoy being with Gretchen this evening," Harri offered, hoping to make amends for her earlier behavior.

"The two of you should have lunch together. Gretchen could use a friend."

Her hand tightened in his as they turned the corner and headed toward the ice cream parlor.

"And your book—what I've seen of it—is very good," she added.

"I know."

She punched him in the ribs. "Egotist!"

Harri didn't let herself think about the way Shae was holding her hand or the feelings it brought to life within her. It had been difficult for her to adjust to single life. Her desires seemed to crop up at the strangest times, reminding her that she was still alive, that she was still a woman who needed to be held in a man's arms and made love to.

As if Shae sensed her needs, his arm dropped to her waist, and he squeezed her affectionately.

Gazing up at him, she smiled. "What's that for?"

"Damned if I know."

Since the ice cream parlor was about to close, they barely had time to make their purchase.

Five minutes after entering the small white building with the colorful, candy-striped awnings, they stepped outside, licking their double-dipped, double dutch, chocolate sugar cones. The walk home was even slower since they had to lick fast to keep the melting ice cream from running down the sides of their hands. Laughing, they paused under a street-light, bantering with each other about who was making the biggest mess.

When they finished their cones, they were still

squabbling over the last napkin as they climbed the steps leading to the Whitlock's massive front porch. Dropping down onto the wooden porch swing, Harri wiped the last of the chocolate off her face.

Shae sat down beside her, and the old chain started to creak as they began to swing. Harri's bare legs brushed against his hair-roughened ones, and somewhere deep inside her a familiar ache began to build.

"What do you think we should do about this?" he asked softly.

Her stomach jumped. It was uncanny the way he could read her thoughts.

It was clear to both of them that there was a strong physical pull between them, a pull that was growing stronger every day.

"I don't know . . . what do you think we should do?"

The swing creaked back and forth, back and forth.

"Well, we could go to your bedroom . . . or mine and do what's been on both our minds all evening."

"Huh-uh," she said with an uneasy toss of her head.

Undaunted, he continued. "Or, we could have a glass of wine . . . maybe take a long shower together. . . ."

"Huh-uh."

Creak, creak, creak.

His hand moved over to rest lightly on top of her bare leg. "After the shower, I could put a little bath powder on you—then you could put some lotion on me."

"Huh-uh."

"And then you could put on that sexy little garter belt you were wearing the other night."

"The cream-colored one?"

"You have others?" His eyes inspected her lazily.

"Uh-huh," she nodded.

"We'll start with the cream-colored one. You have a problem with that?"

"Yep."

He glanced up. "Why?"

"I don't go for one-night stands."

Shifting slightly, he rested his arm across the back of the swing. "Who said anything about a one-night stand?"

"No one, but no one mentioned anything to the contrary."

"Such as?" His hand brushed through her hair.

Harri leaned her head back against his arm, trying to absorb the night's magical aura: the humid scent of roses, the chirping of crickets. "Such as . . . love," she said softly.

"You have to be in love with a man to want to go to bed with him?" he asked softly. His hand moved to gently massage her shoulder, and Harri felt the heat expand in her stomach.

The faint scent of gardenias came to her as she tried to imagine the kind of lover he would be. Passionate, intense, hungry.

It would be shortsighted to sleep with him. She knew that. Yet she longed to lie naked against his warm flesh, to listen to the strong beat of his heart, to bury her face in the rough texture of that glorious hair on his chest.

Her eyes flew open guiltily. The ache inside her was so pronounced that it had become a throbbing agony.

In trying to force that image away, a new, even

more disturbing one rose up to take its place: Shae, stepping out of a shower, toweling dry; Shae slipping into a pair of bikini briefs; Shae lifting her, his eyes darkened with passion as he held her against his length, letting her feel the power of his need. . . .

"You're sure you don't want to think about it?" he persisted.

"Huh-uh," she said shaking her head.

Sobering, he reached out to trace the underside of her jaw with his forefinger. "Harri, I'm leaving in the morning."

Surprised, she lifted her gaze to meet his. "Leaving?"

His eyes probed hers in the ray of moonlight that bathed the old front porch. "Not for long—just for a few weeks."

Frustration filled her and radiated from her eyes. "Why?"

"To finish the book . . . I'll be back in a month or less." The decision had not come easy. He wanted to stay with her, yet he wanted this book behind him. He had to tell her now who he was. Easing his mouth closer, he said softly, "I don't want to go, but I have no choice."

"Why . . . why do you have to go? Can't you finish the book here?"

She knew it was selfish, but she took pride in his book. Though she wanted none of the credit, it was a part of him that he'd shared with her, something he'd never permitted in the past.

And now he wanted to leave and finish the book alone?

"No, I have to go. You know, I haven't been getting anything done . . ."

Their mouths brushed, flooding them with a rush of white heat.

"But I don't want you to go," she murmured, hating herself for being so weak.

"Harri . . ." Her essence washed over him, tormenting him. Crushing her to him, his mouth took hers roughly, and she responded. He could feel her heart pounding, her need matching his.

Unleashed, the passion consumed them. The barriers were down. The game was over.

"Lord, I want you," he murmured huskily between lips that were mindlessly moving over her face, then returning to her mouth to re-acquaint himself with her taste. "Stay with me tonight."

Harri didn't have to be asked again. "Yes . . . oh, yes . . ."

Mindlessly, he plunged his tongue into her mouth, and she responded hungrily. Suddenly nothing else mattered as blind, primitive needs flared to consume them. Desires could no longer be controlled or channeled, only appeased. The old swing abruptly stopped creaking as his arms slid beneath her and he rose to his feet.

Tell her Malone, don't make love to her with this pretense still between you.

But he was powerless to find the words to tell her. A little more time—that's all he needed. Time to explain himself in a way that wouldn't hurt her.

His breath was uneven as he gazed down at her. "Stop me," he pleaded raggedly.

Shaking her head wordlessly, Harri buried her hands in his hair to bring his mouth back to hers, arousing a deeper hunger in him. "Are you sure?" he whispered. He held himself barely in check to gaze into her eyes once more. This decision would be hers. He wanted her. Lord, how he wanted her. More than that, he wanted her to want him, without regrets now or later.

"Very sure." Her voice was firm; her gaze, steady.

He carried her upstairs and into her room. Inside the doorway, he paused as desire raced hot and unchecked through his veins. Their mouths fused together heatedly as he let her body slowly slide against his length until her feet touched the floor. He took one step back and reached to drag her shorts down over her hips. His impatience mounted as the stretch fabric clung to her curves, refusing to yield quickly enough. He swore at first, then let his mouth follow the inching progress, his passion inflamed even more as she arched against him, murmuring his name.

Buttons were forgotten as he ripped aside her blouse, baring the silky wisp of her bra. Lowering his mouth, he tasted the satin swell as his hand fumbled with the clasp. A moment later the lace fell away, and he murmured his approval. Heat suffused him, overpowered him, drove him.

He tasted the faint traces of chocolate still clinging to her mouth, as his lips returned to hers. His arms gathered her close, but he couldn't seem to get close enough. He embraced her like a drowning man. He had wanted a woman before, but never like this.

Suddenly they were both fighting with his clothing, their hands tangling with buttons and snaps. When his briefs dropped to the floor, her hands explored him boldly, longing to know every wonderful, secret part of him.

They fell across her bed as their whispers carried

an unintelligible, meaningless litany of wants and needs.

Rolling over, he drove into her, then he stopped himself as he struggled for a return of some reason and sanity. He was mindless with desire, but he wouldn't hurt her. He hesitated until he felt her yield, until her movements urged him on. Then completely, and without question, he took her.

Moving deeply inside her, he heard her muffled groan against his throat, and he knew her need matched his.

Lord, I'm in love with her, he realized as the pressure built and tore at him. Their bodies touched, caressed, probed, and searched, until mindless with need, he felt the world suddenly burst into a million blinding stars.

As the mists of pleasure gently began to subside, he held her tightly, afraid to let her go. No woman had ever touched him as deeply as she just had.

Dropping his head to her shoulder, he brushed his mouth across her perfumed softness. "I'm sorry . . . I'd hoped to be more in control the first time."

Smiling, she closed her eyes, clasping his head to her breast tightly. "I wouldn't change a moment of what we just shared."

Lifting his head, he kissed the tip of her nose, then her cheeks, then he returned to sample her mouth, still tender from their passion. "Not bad," he said, "for the first time."

She lifted her brows teasingly. "First time? You plan on this happening again?"

"Yeah." His eyes openly adored her as his mouth lowered to take hers again. "You have any problem with that, Whitlock?"

This time, Harriet couldn't think of a one.

Eight

Harri was up long before Shae left the next morning.

Standing before her window, she sipped tasteless coffee as she watched him walk down her front steps. He waved at her briefly before stepping through the hedge. She held her breath as she watched him climb his steps and his door close behind him. She was doing her best to convince herself that he would be back.

He'll only be gone a few weeks, she reasoned. Only a few short weeks. The time would go by before she realized it. But what if he changed his mind and decided to fly back to New York when the book was finished?

No, he couldn't do that. Please, heaven, he couldn't do that.

Last night had been too perfect.

Resting her head against the window frame, she closed her eyes, recalling the way he'd made love to her. His unique scent still lingered around her. She could smell the faint aroma of warm flesh mingling pleasantly with the scent of his cologne, she could still see the way his hair curled crisply at the base of his neck; and she could still feel the texture of his beard on her bare stomach.

It would be weeks before she saw him again. To Harri, that sounded a few days short of a millennium.

But after last night, she had hope. She was gaining ground with him, even though she feared that somewhere in the dark recesses of his mind, he still thought of her as Harriet the Curse.

As she stretched lazily, a smile touched the corners of her mouth. Given enough time, she would make him see her the way she wanted to be: Harri the Unforgettable.

Shae was not a man to be pushed, and she respected that. In fact, that made her love him all the more. When he returned, she would let him set the pace for their growing relationship—meanwhile she'd just pray that the next few weeks would be a turning point in their lives.

He'll miss me, she thought smugly, salving her injured pride with the memory of how many hours he'd caressed her, made love to her, and nestled her close in his arms before he'd finally drifted to sleep. He would be back.

"I'll have my fruit now, thank you."

"Sighing, Harri pulled her thoughts back to the present. "Okay, Myron. You may have two slices of orange today."

While Harri showered and dressed, Magnolia sat on the bed and flipped the channels on the television set back and forth.

While absently listening to Willard Scott predicting that it would be eighty-something today and Ed McMahon instructing Americans to look in their mailbox because they just might be the lucky winners of a ten-million-dollar sweepstakes, Harri slapped hot rollers in her hair and applied her make-up.

When the phone rang, she snatched the remote away from Magnolia and turned the volume down.

"Hello."

"Hi, babe."

"Hi, Mike." She sat down on the side of the bed and held the remote firmly out of Magnolia's reach. Peeved, the monkey began jumping on the bed, standing on her head, then flopping over on her back for attention.

"How would you like to have a three-day, all-expense-paid vacation?"

"I'd love it. When do I leave?"

Mike chuckled. "Don't you even want to know where you're going?"

"Not particularly. The key words are 'all expenses paid.' "

"Well, it's not exactly Bora Bora."

"Exactly what is it?" she bantered.

"Lake Pocataro."

Harri's face fell. "Oh." The resort was nice, but it wouldn't have been her pick of the ideal vacation spot. "What's up?"

"The Zoo Directors' Conference. I'm scheduled to go, but I'm snowed under with this building project so I was hoping you might take pity on me and go in my place."

She frowned. "When?"

"This coming weekend."

Harri thought about the empty house next door and an even emptier next few weeks without Shae.

"You won't be tied up in meetings all day," Mike said. "You'll probably be able to work in a few rounds of golf and a little sunbathing. Think you can tear yourself away from drooling over Malone long enough to make the trip for me?"

"Shae had to leave for awhile," she replied absently, thinking about the offer. Lake Pocataro would be better than sitting around the house all weekend.

"Good, then you can go?"

"Sure Mike, I can go in your place."

"You can?"

She laughed at the relief she heard in his voice. "I don't have anything else to do, but what about the animals?"

"Peg said she would babysit this weekend."

"Peg said *she* would?" Harri laughed again. Peg Miller was close to seventy, the wife of John, the zoo's oldest maintenance man. Neither John nor Peg was known to be particularly fond of animals. "Are you serious?"

"It floored me too but I'm not going to look a gift horse in the mouth."

"Do you think she can handle them?"

"I don't see why not. The animals are doing okay, aren't they?"

"Ricky's still a little under the weather, but he's eating well."

"Peg should be able to handle them, and John will be around. I'll check in on her a couple of times a day, too."

"Whatever you think."

"I'll send some men over to move the cages this morning."

"Okay, I'll pack Myron's oranges."

When Harri hung up, Magnolia scampered back to claim the remote control again.

Handing it back reluctantly, Harri returned to the bathroom.

A moment later, she heard Geraldo interviewing a woman who claimed to have had sex with a ghost. Harri shook her head, grinning back at herself in the mirror. Peg was going to have an enlightening three days.

It rained during the drive to Lake Pocataro Friday afternoon. A hard, driving rain with occasional bolts of lightning, and claps of thunder that rattled her small car.

When Harri finally turned the small Volkswagen into the plush resort late that afternoon, she was almost sorry she had agreed to fill in for Mike.

The way it looked, she was going to be stuck inside a hotel for three long days, watching the rain.

Handing her key to the valet, she gathered her luggage, then walked into the lobby to register.

"I'll have those bags delivered to your room, Ms. Whitlock." Snapping his fingers, the clerk summoned a bellman. "Room two thirty-six."

A few minutes later, Harri accepted the plastic card that would unlock her door and punched the elevator button.

The door opened, and as she started to step inside, a man stepped out and collided with her.

"Oh, sorry—"

"Excuse me—"

They glanced up, stunned, when familiar blue eyes met puzzled amber ones.

"Shae?"

"Harri!"

"What are you doing here?" they exclaimed simultaneously.

Harri's chin automatically lifted. Her tone had conveyed a friendly "what are you doing here?" while his tone had clearly implied "and what are *you* doing here!"

"I'm here on business," she announced, stung by his less than cordial greeting. "And you?"

"Business? You never mentioned a business trip," he said.

"I didn't know it until yesterday!"

"Oh, really?"

His eyes darted around the lobby nervously as he moved her out of the path of others trying to enter the elevator.

Shrugging his hand aside, she let the crowd carry her into the waiting car.

"Where are you going?" he called.

Her nose turned up self-righteously. "To my room." He had not said one word about coming to Lake Pocataro!

Parting the crowd, he took her arm, moving her back out of the car. "Excuse us . . . excuse us . . . excuse me."

"What's the matter with you?" she demanded when they were back in the lobby again. She shook his hand off impatiently.

"Lower your voice," he warned, glancing over his

shoulder uncomfortably. His voice dropped. "I'd rather no one recognized me."

"Recognized you?"

"Harri, keep it down, will you?" Shae reached inside his pocket and removed a pair of dark sunglasses. Slipping them on, he glanced back at her. "We need to talk. Let's go to the bar."

Harri viewed his almost theatrical manner with an open mouth. "*What* are you doing?"

"Harri, let's go to the lounge—"

Shrugging out of his grasp a third time, she straightened. "You don't think that *I* followed you up here, do you?"

His gaze moved around the lobby anxiously as he explained quietly, "I'm not suggesting anything. It just seems odd to me that all of a sudden here we are in the same hotel . . ."

Harri was so angry, so humiliated, so hurt by his thinly veiled assumption that she pushed him aside and stepped into the elevator, her face flaming.

She stood in the lobby, and the occupants of the car waited expectantly as the two antagonists glared at each other.

"I didn't say that you followed me," he said.

"You might as well have. I'm taking it that way."

"Harri, get off that elevator."

Her chin lifted again, and her eyes met his evenly. "Not in a bizillon years."

An uneasy silence followed as the couple continued to defy one another.

"You want me to carry you off?"

"You want to live another day?"

A small man standing in the front row, dressed in

a dark conservative business suit, finally edged forward, smiling apologetically at Shae, "Going up?"

Harri's hand shot up to press the close-door button. "Not in this car, he isn't."

The man was still smiling lamely as the doors shut a moment later.

A tense silence came over the car as it began a slow ascent. Harri kept her eyes straight ahead, trying to blink back tears.

The nerve of him accusing her of following him! Who does that jerk think he is? Some hot shot celebrity who has to hide from the public? Putting on those silly sunglasses and muttering under his breath that he didn't want to be recognized. We need to talk, Harri, he says. The man is beginning to sound like a broken record!

When the doors slid open on the second floor, Shae was outside the elevator door waiting for her.

The little man hurriedly jumped aside as Harri swept out of the car. Ignoring Shae, she walked down the hallway, key in hand.

"Aren't we acting a little juvenile about this?" he said as she squinted to read the numbers on each door. She'd left her prescription glasses in the car and wasn't wearing her contacts, so finding her room seemed practically hopeless.

"How did you know what floor I was on?" she demanded.

"I know the desk clerk."

"I'm going to complain to the manager that the employees are giving out privileged information."

She paused before a door, and looking very much like Mr. Magoo, struggled to read the numbers. After several attempts, she managed to insert the plastic card into the lock, then she rattled the door knob and tried to get the flashing light to come on.

"You will not report this to the desk clerk," Shae ordered from behind her.

"Watch me." She jiggled the card. "If you think for one minute that I've chased you up here, you're sadly mistaken. I was just as surprised to see you as you were to see me. If you had told me you were coming to Lake Pocataro, I wouldn't have come within fifty miles of here."

Frustrated, she slapped her palms against the door angrily. A second later, the door flew open and a wild-haired man with his shirttail hanging out of his pants glared back at her. "What in the hell is going on?" he bellowed.

Shocked, she stepped back. "I . . . is this room two thirty-six?"

"No!" The door slammed in her face.

Moving on down the hallway, she paused before another door. Glancing at Shae, she snapped, "Is this two thirty-six?" She was close to tears.

Relieved, she felt Shae remove the card from her hand. A moment later, the door opened, and he guided her inside.

As she opened her mouth to protest, he swiftly drew her into his arms. Confused, she let herself lean against him as his mouth took hers hungrily.

The faint scent of his after-shave tantalized her as she heard him groan with male appreciation. His tongue searched for hers, as he settled her more tightly against his length.

Severing the kiss, she drew back from him. "Stop it, Shae. In case you haven't noticed, I'm a little put out with you at the moment—Shae!"

Ignoring the buttons on her blouse, he began to pull it over her head.

"Shae, I'm warning you—" Her words were cut off as his mouth came down on hers again.

Flipping the lock on the door, his hands came back to caress the soft skin between her bra and skirt.

"Just calm down," he said soothingly, barely letting her catch her breath between kisses. "I'm sorry if I acted like a jerk earlier."

"You did. A big one—and I didn't chase you up here. I thought after the night we spent together you would realize that I am not the Harriet from your childhood, the Harriet who'd do anything to trick you."

"I realized that weeks ago—easy sweetheart . . ." His mouth made a lazy foray down the side of her neck, pausing to nibble at her shoulders. "I want to make love, Harri, not war." Her breath caught as his hand began to caress her breast.

"Shae, you make me crazy . . . if you think because of one night in the moonlight I'll just jump into bed with you every time you snap your fingers—"

His mouth traveled back up the length of her neck, stilling her with a soft whisper in her ear. "I want to make you crazy . . . I want to make you so crazy that you can't think of anything or anyone else but me."

Unhooking her bra, he captured the pliant flesh in the palms of his hands.

A flash of lightning illuminated the room as the rain started to come down outside again. A moment later, the low rumble of thunder seemed to enclose the room with a dark intimacy. His mouth demanded a response from hers, and she found herself a willing victim.

Settling closer to his masculine length, she felt his fingers work the snap on her skirt as his mouth closed over hers again with a searing urgency.

The anger slowly drained from her as the heat inside her began to build.

"Shae . . . can't permit this happen when you think I've followed you here," she murmured helplessly. "I have more pride than that."

"It doesn't matter if you did." He began lowering her skirt over her hips. When the lightweight fabric dropped to the floor, his hand dipped below her garter belt and slipped into her panties, to caress her naked thigh. "You've been on my mind constantly since I arrived. I came up here to work, but I find that all I can do is think about you."

Groaning, he moved his fingers to the snaps on her waist. "Well look what we have here . . . the garter belt." His breath was like warm wine against her ear.

"Now I feel guilty again—I didn't wear this to distract you."

"Ah, but you do distract me," he whispered, his mouth taking hers again hotly.

The last of her restraint melted as his hands became bold and probing.

As he eased her toward the bed, she stopped resisting him.

A clap of thunder shook the room as she reached for the buttons on his shirt, a mute concession that she wanted him as badly as he wanted her. Peeling the fabric away, she lay her head against his chest, drinking in his scent. Tilting her head back, her gaze moved from him to the bed. As usual, he read her mind.

Easing her toward the mattress, he found her shaking her head.

"No?"

"Not there. Not this time," she said softly.

Grinning, he lifted her chin. "Oh?"

She gazed at him, her longing exposed. "Do you mind?"

"Hell no, I don't mind," he murmured, as his mouth came back to meet hers. They kissed with a building hunger, his desire rose, firm and unyielding, as lightning illuminated the room again.

She loosened his belt and opened the zipper. Peeling the denim over his hips, she eased his jeans, along with his briefs, down his legs, kneeling to run her tongue around the area of his navel.

She heard his sharp intake of breath as he drew her face against his belly, holding her until the resulting tremors subsided.

Rising, she kissed her way back up his bare torso, then she paused to guide his hands to her thighs to unhook her silk hose. Slowly, he drew each nylon down her long shapely legs, letting his fingertips play lightly over her knees and calves. Their eyes met, clouded now by passion as he removed the last lacy obstacle.

He stood before her, powerful and awesome in his need. Their breathing became as one as they gazed into each other's eyes.

"Have I mentioned that I'm in love with you, Harriet Whitlock?" he whispered softly.

Harri could feel her body growing lighter. "No, Shae Malone, I don't believe you have."

"I haven't? You sure?" His tongue lowered to tease hers provocatively.

"I think I would have remembered if you had."

Gazing deeply into her eyes, he said softly, "Well, lady, you'd better hold on to your hat because you and I are about to become better acquainted."

Easing her against the wall, he braced his arms above her head. Slowly, he leaned his body flush against hers.

Slipping her hand lower, she found him. "Oh, yeah?"

Pressing her more solidly against the wall, he eased into her, murmuring hoarsely, "Oh, yeah . . ."

Nine

A noise outside the room woke Harri early the next morning. She rolled over to nestle closer against Shae. Stirring, he drew her into his arms, kissing her as he drifted back to sleep. The rattle of a breakfast cart and the sound of water running overhead melted her drowsiness.

Last night they had left her room for a late supper. Afterward, they had returned to his room where they'd spent the night.

She snuggled closer to his bare chest as memories of the night before flooded her with contentment. She recalled the passion, the gentleness, the mutual hunger they had shared.

It had never been that way with Patrick. She'd always been aware that something vital and alive was missing in their relationship, and now she knew what that was.

She had loved her husband, but not the way she loved Shae.

She could never remember a time in her life when she hadn't loved Shae. From the day they met as toddlers, she had idolized him.

Her mouth curved sleepily at the memory of those turbulent years. It had been a wonder that Shae hadn't run away from home to rid himself of her. But he hadn't. Though he'd resented her shameless pursuit, he had hung in there and been man enough to endure it.

Her hand gently caressed the outline of his buttocks as he slept, marveling at the sense of completeness she had found in his arms.

It had been close to dawn when they had finally dropped into an exhausted sleep. They had made love for hours, unable to appease their appetites.

She squeezed his waist gently, and he stirred again.

Her eyes drifted shut as she dared to dream that one day he might ask her to marry him. Of course, she would accept.

Until his first book was published, they would have to struggle like any other young couple striving to make ends meet, but she would be willing to live in a tar paper shack if she had to. She'd make any sacrifice to be with him.

She would continue working until they decided to have a baby, and by then, he should be established.

If his book was never published, then she figured that he could always buy some small retail business, and she could help him run it.

Maybe that would be even better than having him published, she reasoned. Though she'd never met a published writer, she assumed that being in such a competitive field would be difficult.

Having to deal with deadlines, rejections, and having his work continually open to criticism could put a dent in even the heartiest ego.

She felt a twinge of jealousy. If Shae were to become famous, she would have to share him with the world—maybe even other women. Her eyes opened slowly at the disturbing thought. Well, she didn't plan on doing that; she'd worked too hard to get him.

Beginning this morning, she was going to start playing down the importance of that silly book he was working on. As soon as her parents returned from Europe she would ask her father to suggest a good, sound business venture.

Giving Shae another affectionate squeeze around the middle again, she sighed. Maybe owning his own book store would make him happy. She squeezed him again, glad she'd thought of it.

Stirring for a third time, Shae sat halfway up, cocking a sleepy eye at her. "Huh?"

He had been squeezed so many times he was beginning to feel like an overripe melon at the market.

"Nothing, darling," she murmured. "Go back to sleep."

Mumbling, he drifted off again.

Realizing she was too excited to sleep, Harri slipped out of bed and went into the bathroom. Her first meeting wasn't scheduled until later that morning, so she had time for a brisk swim.

Coming out of the bathroom a few minutes later, she found that Shae was still sound asleep. Glancing at the clock, she saw that it was barely seven. Deciding to let him sleep, she leaned over the bed and kissed him on his stubbly cheek. "I'm going to my room to change, sleepyhead. Then maybe I'll go for a swim."

Murmuring his sleepy permission, he rolled over and pulled the pillow over his head.

A half hour later, Harri stepped out of the elevator into the lobby, humming. A few early-morning travelers were dragging luggage to the front entrance to be loaded into airport shuttles.

The smell of fresh-perked coffee drew her in the direction of the large urn set up on a long, cloth-covered table in the lobby. An assortment of sweet rolls and croissants were being offered to appease the early risers.

Stepping up to the registration desk, Harri waited until the clerk had finished checking out a departing guest. Turning, he smiled at her. "Good morning."

"Good morning. Please hold all calls to room five twenty-six until after ten o'clock," she requested.

The clerk reached for a pen. "Yes, ma'am. Room five twenty-six—Shae's room?" He glanced up to look at her again. "Shae wants his calls held until after ten?"

"Yes, Mr. Malone was up very late last night, and he's sleeping in this morning."

The clerk chuckled as he wrote the message on a pad. "These writers—they try to burn the candle at both ends, don't they?"

Harri smiled. "Yes, Shae works much too hard."

"Well," he ripped the message off the pad. "I guess it pays off. You read his latest?"

Harri smiled. "No . . . he doesn't let anyone read his work."

The clerk glanced up blankly. "He doesn't?"

"No, he thinks it's bad luck to let anyone read a manuscript before it's finished."

"Right." He chuckled. "We should all have Perry Beal's bad luck."

"Isn't that the truth." Flashing him a friendly grin, she turned to leave.

She had gotten two-thirds of the way to the coffee urn when it dawned on her what the clerk had said.

Perry Beal's luck? What's that supposed to mean?

Her pace slowed as she turned to glance back at the clerk.

Perry Beal's luck?

Making a wide circle, she sauntered back to the desk. The clerk looked up and smiled. "Something else?"

"Yes . . . exactly what did you mean when you said, 'We should all have Perry Beal's luck?' "

"Oh, well, I meant don't we all wish we had Shae's luck," he said.

"What's Shae's luck have to do with Perry Beal?"

The young man grinned. "You don't know?"

"I don't know."

His face suddenly drained of all color. "Excuse me, I thought . . . aren't you here with Shae?"

"No." Her heart began to pound. "I'm here with the zoo directors' conference."

The clerk glanced around the lobby, then leaning forward, he pleaded in an anxious whisper, "Please, forget that I said *anything.*"

Harri leaned closer. "Anything? About what?"

"About Shae Malone being Perry Beal."

"Shae Malone is Perry Beal," she repeated in a flat tone.

The clerk was speaking clearly enough, but his words were failing to register.

The clerk glanced anxiously over his shoulder again. "Please, ma'am, I could lose my job over this," he confided in a hoarse whisper. "I just assumed you were with Shae, so . . ."

"No, I'm not . . . but don't worry about your job," Harri said distractedly.

She turned, her feet moving woodenly toward the pool.

Shae is Perry Beal.

Perry Beal—one of the most successful young authors in publishing. *Her idol—Perry Beal.*

Crossing the lobby in a daze, she struggled to absorb the shocking news.

Shae is Perry Beal.

As the meaning of the words finally began to sink in, Harri was flooded by a tide of anger. Cold, merciless anger.

He'd been lying to her, making her think he was a struggling, unpublished writer, all this time, while he was the author of five, best-selling mystery novels.

Why? Why had he let her make such a fool of herself?

Because he is playing with you, Harriet. He's afraid that if you know the truth, he will never get rid of you, Harriet the Curse.

Blinded by tears now, she pushed through the glass door, the knowledge too painful to absorb. The pool lay shimmering like blue topaz beneath the morning sun, but Harri didn't notice. Blind, cold fury threatened to consume her.

How he must have laughed at her. She remembered how she had given him a list of ideas, how she had demanded that he strengthen his characterization, trying to teach him how to breathe life into *his* story.

Oh, he must have been in stitches at that one. Sinking down on the nearest chair, she buried her face in her hands, heartsick. She wasn't sure if it was her pride or her heart that hurt the most, but one thing was crystal clear: She could never forgive him for humiliating her this way. This was too much.

Harri Whitlock was no longer the love-struck teenager who would willingly forgive Shae Malone anything just to gain his favor. There was considerably more at stake than a thirteen-year-old's infatuation.

At thirteen, she hadn't gone to bed with him.

Tears began to stream from the corners of her eyes as she realized that she had played straight into his hands again last night.

Harriet Whitlock was the same mindless robot, still chasing after him. He'd had his laugh. It had taken him fifteen years to do it, but he had finally paid her back for all the times that she had made his life miserable.

Swiping angrily at her tears with the backs of her hands, she tried to gain control of her emotions, but memories of the night she'd just spent making love to Shae—pouring her heart out, telling him how much she loved him—had always loved him, was tearing her apart.

Now that his ego had been stroked, he could return to New York to brag to all his Friday night drinking buddies about what he'd done to ole' gullible Harriet!

Well, Mr. Hot Shot Malone, you may have had

your fun, but ole' Harriet is going to have the last laugh.

Rising, she wiped the corners of her eyes with the tail of her cover-up and marched back into the lobby.

The same clerk glanced up and paled when he saw her coming.

"Ring Mr. Malone's room, please."

"What?"

"Ring five twenty-six," she repeated firmly.

"I thought you wanted me to hold Mr. Malone's calls—"

"I said *five twenty-six, right now!*"

"*Yes, ma'am!*" He shot her an anxious look as he reached for the phone.

It rang four times before Shae finally rolled over to answer it. "Yes?"

The clerk handed the receiver to Harri. "Hi, darling," she said breezily. "Did I wake you?"

Shae glanced at the clock on the bedstand. "Harri? Where are you?"

"In the lobby, sweetheart. I just had a wonderful idea!"

Dropping his head back on the pillow, Shae tried to clear the cobwebs out of his mind.

"Are you listening, darling?" she asked cheerfully.

"Yeah . . . you have a wonderful idea."

"It's about your book."

One eye opened warily. "Yes?"

"I've just had a brainstorm on how you can end it."

Shae yawned, scratching his head. "Yeah?"

"Yes, you see I thought that you could have your heroine—oh, Shae, this is so good I can't do it justice over the phone. Meet me at the swimming beach in fifteen minutes."

Shae glanced at the clock again. "Harri . . . it's seven-fifteen, sweetheart," he said, "as in early in the morning seven-fifteen."

"I know what time it is, but this is important . . . you do want the book to sell, don't you?"

"Harri—look, I've been meaning to talk to you about—"

"Oh, not now, Shae. Later, darling. Fifteen minutes. I'll be waiting for you . . . and Shae, wear your bathing suit."

Coming fully awake now, Shae grinned. "You insatiable little wench." She had been incredible last night, the kind of woman he could easily spend the rest of his life with. He was crazy in love with Harriet Whitlock, and now he could admit it to anyone—even to himself. "If you're so eager, why don't you just come back to the room and—"

"Fifteen minutes, Shae," she interrupted. A moment later, the line went dead.

Hopping out of bed, Shae stretched, beat on his chest energetically, and headed for the shower.

This was going to be one hell of a day!

The two mile stretch of shoreline behind Pocataro Lodge was completely deserted at this hour. Harri paced up and down the sandy beach, rehearsing what she was going to say to him.

Muttering under her breath, she pointed, jabbed, and gritted her teeth with disgust as she let the miserable wretch have it with both barrels.

She hoped he was pleased with himself. She hoped

he was happy now. He'd made a fool out of her; he had humiliated her, and he had put her in her place.

She began to mutter out loud, "Are you happy now? You are. Well, wonderful! But let me tell you something, mister—" Harri glanced up and saw a lone figure jogging down the beach toward her. Her eyes narrowed as she recognized the familiar thatch of red hair.

Well, well, here came Jaws, moving in for the kill.

She straightened, running her hand through her wind-blown hair as if it mattered how a bonehead looked.

Shae waved, and she lifted her hand and waved back.

Offering him her brightest smile, she watched as he approached her, counting to ten under her breath to stifle the urge to murder him with her bare hands.

"Hi." Shae paused before her, reaching out to draw her to him for a long good-morning kiss.

Willing herself to permit this atrocity, she shut her eyes and suffered through it.

You jackass, you moron, you conniving, deceitful, manipulative, sneaky, deceptive, dishonest, insidious—

After long moments, Shae broke the kiss, drawing back to look at her. "You okay, honey?"

She smiled. "Of course, darling. Why do you ask?"

Draping his arm around her, they began to walk. "Why did you leave so early?" He gazed down at her with those lovely blue eyes that she would love to jab out. "I thought we might take our time getting out of bed this morning."

"Oh, really?" she said evenly. "That would have been nice."

"Nice?" He drew her closer. "Having you in my bed for the rest of the day would be paradise."

"Oh, Shae." She paused, turning on her tiptoes to wrap her arms around his neck. "You should have said something, sweetheart." Dragging his mouth back to hers, they exchanged another long kiss.

Lord, she was kissing Perry Beal—*the* Perry Beal! For a moment the thought threatened her composure, but she reminded herself that he was also Shae Malone, and then she found the courage to go on.

As their lips finally parted and they rubbed noses affectionately, the heady scent of his after-shave filled her senses. "After our swim," he murmured, "there's no law that says we can't go back to bed."

"Sounds wonderful," she purred. "But I bet you're excited about my idea?" she whispered against his lips.

"Well, I'm excited about something, all right."

"About the book?"

"That too. Now, Harri—" he draped his arm around her again, and they started down the beach, "—about my book—"

"The idea hit me like a ton of bricks," she interrupted. Pausing again, she turned him to face her, letting her hands slide through the thick patch of hair on his chest. "Now, picture this: The heroine thinks it's the stepbrother who's killed her father, but she can't prove it. So—" her hand slid down to rest on the front part of his bathing suit that was already showing signs of strain— "she decides to seduce the half-brother in an attempt to wring a confession from him."

Shae smiled, stepping closer as her hand began to wander. "I like this already. But the sister-in-law committed the crime, remember?"

"I know, but just to throw the reader off course, let's let them believe that it's conceivable that the step-brother had a part in it. So, calling him early one morning, the heroine invites the step-brother to this secluded stretch of beach for a swim."

A knowing smile shadowed the corners of Shae's mouth. "Right," he said huskily, moving closer. "And?"

Harri glanced around to make sure they were still alone. "Being a man, he agrees—"

"Now, wait a minute. I can't suggest to my readers that just because he's a man he would necessarily agree—"

His words faltered as her hand slipped inside the front of his suit. "Relax, darling, I'm just being suggestive."

Grinning, he locked her hand in place. "And how— but take your time. I'm in no hurry."

His mouth lowered to take hers again. A moment later, he whispered, "Would Chantel be doing this to Maximilian so quickly?"

Pressing closer to him, she rotated her hips slowly against his. "What do you think?"

"I think I want to go back to the room. Now."

Her hands slipped to his waistband and began to slowly lower his suit.

Shae's hand shot out to stop her in a halfhearted protest. "Easy, sweetheart. We're on a public beach—"

"All alone."

He chuckled with masculine certainty, which caused Harri to dig her nails into his waist.

"Ouch!"

"Oh, sorry." She smiled as her hands resumed their task. "Well, anyway, Chantel gets Maximilian alone, and she begins to undress him, her eyes filled with unbridled lust."

"Unbridled lust."

"Yes—unbridled—totally *unbridled.*"

His suit slid down his legs and settled around his ankles.

Shae glanced around, still uneasy about the place she had chosen for this seduction. "Hey, I don't want to dampen your mood . . . but shouldn't we find a little privacy—"

Leaning over, she jerked the suit under his feet, nearly tripping him in her haste. "Don't be silly. There isn't anyone around."

His hands moved to shield his masculinity. He wasn't overly modest, but on a public beach in broad daylight?

"Now that Chantel has Maximilian at her mercy," she continued, ignoring his apprehensive glances over his shoulder; she edged closer, pushing his hands aside, "Chantel shows her true colors. She realizes Maximilian has made a fool of her, and she resents it! Coaxing the truth out of him isn't good enough. She wants him to *pay* for what he's done. And pay *dearly.*"

"Yeah," he said, distracted by the movement of her hands on his flesh, deciding to play along for the moment. "And Maximilian tells her to make him pay and pay and pay . . ."

"I couldn't have said it better." Averting her face

to avoid his kiss, Harri went on in a deadly calm voice, "And then Chantel tucks Maximilian's bathing suit neatly beneath her arm." She smiled. "Then Chantel says—now read my lips carefully, Shae. 'Maximilian, you are a low-down, conniving, no good jackass. You've been lying to me, and no matter how gullible I've been in the past, I don't appreciate being made a fool.'"

Harri's voice had suddenly changed. Recognizing the subtle difference, the smile on Shae's face began to fade. "Too strong," he said, "maybe we should have them make love before the climactic scene."

Harri's smile disappeared. "Let's not. Let's let Chantel retain just a piece of her dignity, and just quietly walk away with his bathing suit tucked under her arm, leaving the poor depraved soul, buck naked—not strapped to the town clock, mind you, but pretty *em-barr-assed*," she enunciated plainly. "No pun intended."

Turning, Harri began to walk away from him.

Shae watched her slack-jawed, her words momentarily failing to register. "Hey . . . wait a minute . . . where are you going?"

"I'm going home, Mr. Beal."

Mr. Beal? Shae's heartbeat accelerated. Oh, hell. Who had told her?

Springing forward, he shouted, "Harri, wait a minute—now, I can explain . . ."

Breaking into a run, Harri fought scalding tears as she called back over her shoulder, "A little late for that, aren't you, Mr. Two-faced Malone?"

"Harri—honey—listen—I've been trying to tell you the truth for weeks. You have to believe me! I just haven't been able to find the right time or we've been distracted—Harri, come back here!"

Harri's feet flew across the sand. "Go to hell, Shae!" She wasn't one to resort to profanity, but those words expressed her feelings exactly.

"Harri! Bring my suit back here! You can't leave me here like this! This isn't funny!"

How was he supposed to get back to the hotel? His eyes darted about frantically as he watched the scrap of blue flapping beneath her arm.

"Nor did I find your deceit so funny!" she tossed back, her voice choked with tears. "Poor old stupid Harriet," she sobbed. "You must have had some laugh!"

"I didn't laugh at you—Harri, I fell in love you—deeply in love with you!"

Harri ran faster, tears streaming down her cheeks. Helpless, Shae watched her go. "Harri, please, sweetheart, I know you're upset but at least let me try to explain! I've tried to tell you—I just couldn't find a way without hurting you—"

Throwing his pride to the wind, he plunged after her until suddenly he spotted an elderly couple coming down the beach. He stopped and whirled. In a flash, he was sprinting in the opposite direction.

"Harri, this is downright rotten!" he muttered as he scrambled over a small rise.

Harri raced toward the elderly couple with Shae's suit flapping under her arm.

"Good morning," she called out as she drew even with them.

They smiled, puzzled. "Good morning."

Looking down the beach, the couple frowned as

they saw a nude man scrambling frantically over a large sand dune.

"Anything wrong, dear?" the man turned and called to the fleeing young woman.

"Just my whole life!" Harri said as she raced on.

Just her whole miserable life!

Ten

"Sorry, it's just me, again, Ms. Whitlock."

The young girl from Jenny's Flowers smiled apologetically at Harri as she handed her another large crate of flowers. It was the delivery girl's third visit to 6430 Sheridan Drive that day.

Wedging a donut into her mouth, Harri reached for a dollar bill lying on the hall table and tucked it into the pocket of the girl's shirt. "Thank you, Celia."

"Want me to do the same thing I've done with all the others?"

"Yes, set them on Mr. Malone's front lawn."

Celia eyed the ten dozen red American Beauty roses and sighed. "Most women are happy to get one dozen roses. This is your fifth crate today, and you've refused to accept any of them."

Harri removed the donut, her fifth that day, and smiled. "Well, as they say, who can predict a woman's whims?"

"Aren't you even curious about what the cards say?"

"I know what the cards say."

Forgive me, I love you, I was wrong.

Shae's messages had arrived in a steady stream for weeks, accompanied by lavish bouquets of white clover, *think of me;* forget-me-not, *true love, forget me not;* heliotrope, *devotion and faithfulness;* jonquils, *I desire a return of affection;* lily-of-the-valley, *return of happiness;* pansies, *thinking of you;* roses, red and white, *unity,* red only, *love.*

The morning the five dozen zinnias had arrived, Harri was puzzled until she picked up the book containing the language of flowers and discovered their message: *thoughts of a friend.* Removing one of the pungent flowers from the vase, she cradled the blossom against her breast and sobbed for another casualty of the war.

Celia sighed. "Okay, but Mr. Malone isn't going to like it. His lawn is beginning to look like a cemetery on Memorial Day."

"Mr. Malone isn't at home."

Five weeks had gone by since the day she had walked out on him at Lake Pocataro.

He had called—as many as five times a day—and left messages on her answering machine, but she had never returned his calls.

The pain of how he had deceived her was still too new, too debilitating to accept.

Closing the door, Harri wondered how long it was going to take him to get her message: fool me once, shame on you; fool me twice, shame on me.

Still, the past few weeks had been the darkest of her life, bleaker than when she'd lost Patrick . . . and that realization hurt her even more.

Why should she waste an ounce of her energy, or

even a single tear, over a man who had deliberately hurt her, a man who cared so little for her feelings that he had continued to let her make an absolute fool of herself?

Every time she thought of the way she had coached him, encouraged him, lain awake at night, racking her brain for a new twist to make his book unique—more marketable—well, it was cruel of him. It was just plain cruel for him to have let her go on believing that she was helping him.

This time, he had gone too far. She knew she had said that before, but this time she meant it. It was high time that she gave up and accepted the fact that she would never be anything in Shae Malone's eyes but hopelessly immature Harriet Whitlock.

Myron shuffled around on his perch restlessly, craning his neck to peer out of the window. "Where's Shae, Big Mama?"

"Shae's gone," Harri said softly.

"Oh—too bad."

The bird's head snapped around to look at her, leaving Harri with the eerie impression that he'd understood her answer and responded to it.

"Yeah." Harri's gaze drifted toward the window wistfully. "Too bad."

The doorbell rang early Saturday evening while Harri was still rummaging through the bottom of her closet looking for the mate to her black pump.

The bell rang twice more before she finally located the missing shoe. Hurrying down the hallway with a lopsided gait, she checked her appearance in each mirror she passed.

Her eyes resembled two burnt holes in a blanket from all the bawling she'd been doing lately, but otherwise she looked okay.

As she reached out to open the door, she vowed she was going to do her best to make the evening pleasant for Mike. She had been terrible company lately, but he had been unusually patient with her, even forgiving her for walking out on the zoo directors' conference.

Pulling the door open, she found Mike standing before her, holding a florist's box, and looking very handsome in his black tie and tux.

His stared back at her, whistling softly through his teeth, "Holy Moley."

Harri smiled, doing a slow pirouette for him. "I take that to mean I have your approval?"

Mike's eyes traveled over the low-cut, backless black evening gown and he smiled. "In a dress like that, you can have anything you want from me."

Handing her the florist's box, he watched as she opened it and removed an exquisite white gardenia.

Lifting the fragrant blossom to her nose, she breathed deeply of the sweet, heady scent. "Thank you. How did you know that gardenias are my favorite?" she murmured, fighting back the memories of the night Shae had first made love to her.

The scent of gardenias had been in the air that night too.

Mike casually picked up the black lace shawl lying on the hall table and draped it around her shoulders. "I appreciate your coming to the benefit dance tonight. I know you've been having a rough time lately, kiddo." He squeezed her shoulders reassuringly.

With trembling fingers, she pinned the flower in

her hair. "I'm sorry, Mike—I know I've been a wretched mess lately."

"Well, if you are, you're the most beautiful mess I've ever met."

Swallowing her tears, she tried to tell herself that maybe she could make herself fall in love with him if he would remove that "Honk, If You're Horny" bumper sticker from his car.

As they backed out of the drive a few minutes later, Harri refused to look at the house next door. The dark interior gave her a feeling of doom.

"By the way. I think you should know—Shae's going to be there tonight."

Harri glanced up. "What?"

Mike adjusted the rearview mirror, avoiding her eyes. "Shae's going to be at the dance tonight."

Turning her head to stare out the window, Harri forced back the large lump forming in her throat. She struggled to convince herself that it didn't matter; they were bound to bump into each other eventually. Living in a community as small as Cloverdale, she had to expect that.

Aware of the strained silence, Mike said softly, "Can you handle it?"

"Of course I can handle it."

"In view of the large donation he's offering, I don't see—"

She turned to face him again. "What donation?"

Mike glanced at her sheepishly. "You haven't heard?"

"Heard what?"

"Malone has offered to donate a hundred thousand to the zoo."

Harri's mouth dropped open. "A hundred thousand —dollars?"

"Pretty impressive, huh? Malone being Perry Beal, the famous mystery writer? Hard to believe, isn't it?"

Harri wasn't listening. Her mind was churning with resentment. A hundred thousand dollars! Shae was offering to make a donation of a hundred thousand dollars to the zoo. And she had paid his way everywhere they went because she thought he was flat broke! The irony of it made her feel sick.

"There is one small stipulation."

Harri kept her eyes straight ahead. "I'll bet. With Shae, there always is."

"He wants one dance with you tonight."

"He'd come closer to seeing me spit horse flies," she snapped.

"Come on, Harri, I know that you and Shae are not exactly bosom buddies at the moment, but do you think it's wise to let your pride stand in the way of such a hefty donation? Think of what it would mean to the zoo. We might even be able to get the bear exhibition underway."

"If Shae wants to dance with someone from the zoo, I'll arrange a dance with Peggy."

"I don't think Peggy is exactly who he has in mind."

They rode in silence for a moment, then Mike repeated softly, "A hundred thousand dollars, Harri. Think about it. One dance—three minutes of your time—a hundred thousand dollars."

"Forget it, Mike. I wouldn't spit on Shae Malone if he erupted in flames."

Mike shook his head, clearly disappointed by her attitude. "You're making a mistake. I don't know what the man has done to you, but he's clearly trying to make amends."

Harri chose not to answer, but she couldn't dismiss Shae's generosity so easily. Having an unexpected hundred thousand dollars dangled as bait was hard to ignore.

While Mike was parking his car and they were walking into the posh dinner club, she thought about what the donation could mean. They could make vast improvements: new signs, walkways and fencing, with enough left over to open the plains portion of the African Area. With that much revenue, they might even be able to put new landscaping around the bathroom areas.

When they entered the crowded dining area, a young hostess stepped forward to greet them, then led them to a large round table at the head of the room.

During dinner, Harri chatted with the chairman of the board, Frank Anderson, and his wife, Arlena, trying her best to keep her mind off Shae's offer.

A hundred thousand dollars. Harri couldn't imagine having that much money, much less giving such an amount away. But then money would be the last thing Perry Beal had to worry about, she fumed.

When ten o'clock arrived, and the benevolent benefactor had failed to appear, Harri began to relax.

He wasn't coming. He didn't have the guts to face her after what he'd done. She wasn't sure if she felt relieved or even angrier. Angrier, she decided, when ten-thirty arrived, and he still wasn't there.

He was toying with her again, baiting her, dangling a hundred thousand dollars under her nose this time to prove that he could still make her jump when he snapped his fingers.

He just couldn't get it through his stubborn ego that his days of manipulating good ole sappy Harriet were over.

"May I have this dance, pretty lady?"

Harri turned at the sound of the deep, masculine voice and smiled. "I'd be honored, Frank."

She moved out onto the dance floor with the white-haired chairman of the board, determined to salvage what was left of the evening. She had paid ninety-five dollars for this dress, and she was going to reap its harvest.

Their feet began to move effortlessly around the floor as the band swung into a lively fox trot.

For the next hour, Harri drifted from one set of arms to the next, deliberately keeping her mind a blank. Shae isn't coming, she told herself over and over again, but her eyes still strayed to the doorway a hundred times more often than they should have.

Around midnight, the band leader stepped to the microphone. "All right, ladies and gentlemen, this is the last one of the evening, a special request for a certain young lady."

Harri sighed and turned to fit herself into Mike's arms, but found a stronger pair waiting for her.

"I believe this one is mine."

Lifting her eyes slowly, she met an achingly familiar pair of blue eyes.

Wordlessly, Shae moved her out onto the dance floor, his gaze relentlessly holding hers as the violins began to play "Strangers In The Night."

Harri could feel her pulse starting to throb as the

lights dimmed, and the silver ball overhead cast a million tiny stars across the dance floor.

Every fiber within her was aware of the man holding her: the smell of his cologne, the uncompromising red in his hair. He looked breathtakingly handsome, wearing a black tux and a powder blue shirt that made his eyes an even more arresting blue.

I've lost him forever, but then, Harri, you can't lose what you've never had.

He drew her closer, his gesture intended to cradle her head against his shoulder. Harri waited until her quickened pulse had steadied, then she said curtly, "Not so close."

His only response was to pull her closer.

The smell of the gardenia washed over him as he closed his eyes and held her, recalling the night they had first made love. There had been gardenias in the air that night too.

The whisper of her gown against the polished dance floor, the warmth of her body pressed against his, the soft strains of the violin—it was all he could do to keep from dropping to his knees and begging her to forgive him.

The past five weeks had been the longest in his life, the most empty, the most meaningless. If he'd had even the slightest doubt that he was in love with this woman, the past few weeks would have served to remove every trace.

"You look beautiful," he whispered, his breath warm against her ear. He had thought of her every moment of every day, and the nights had been unbearable.

Dismayed, she found her eyes filling with tears.

He urged her to look at him, and she saw that his

eyes were misty too. "Are you ready to listen my side of the story?" he asked softly.

"No."

"I love you."

Although she had dreamed of hearing him say those three words to her, she refused to acknowledge them now.

"Don't do this to us, Harri."

Averting her gaze, she refused to answer.

Lowering his head, he nuzzled the side of her neck, kissing her lightly behind her ear as they moved around the floor. "Did Mike mention my offer to make a donation to the zoo?"

"He did." Her tone was steely.

"And you're agreeable?"

"We're dancing, aren't we?"

"You're at liberty to refuse," he reminded, running his tongue around the lobe of her ear. He felt her body begin to tremble in his arms. "Is that what you want?"

"Yes."

Perturbed, she felt his tongue darting into her ear, sending goosebumps racing along her spine.

Jerking her head away, she kept her eyes stubbornly fixed over his shoulder. She would not permit him to wear down her resistance—not for two hundred thousand dollars.

Pausing, he gently took her face in his hands and in a husky whisper informed her, "In view of what this is costing us, the least you can do is see that one of us enjoy it."

"Costing *us*? It's costing me nothing, Mr. Malone."

"Yes it is. The hundred thousand dollar donation is coming out of the advance on the book."

She blinked back hot tears. "Your book—not mine."

He cupped her chin gently. "Our book."

Her eyes met his resentfully. "If you think you can buy your way back into my—"

His mouth lowered again to brush back and forth across hers.

Closing her eyes, Harri felt her knees becoming weak. She went hot, then cold, then numb as she felt his tongue moving along the lower inside of her mouth.

She knew if she responded, showed even the slightest hint that he was getting to her, she would be giving into him again. Bracing herself, she allowed his exquisite torture to continue. Pressing her closer, he allowed the heat of his body to flow through hers.

Pushing away, she averted her gaze. "One dance, Mr. Malone. I did not consent to let you maul me."

"I'm sorry. The bargain was one dance." His mouth took hers swiftly, hungrily.

Groaning, she sagged against him for support, feeling her body growing warm and heavy as involuntary tremors of arousal began to betray her.

Feeling her response, he severed the kiss and whispered urgently against her ear, "In thirty seconds the music is going to end and my time will be up, so you'd better listen, and listen well. At first, I didn't tell you that I was Perry Beal for a purely selfish, childish, egotistical reason. I was scared—scared as hell that if you knew who I was, you'd chase me again and I wouldn't have a minute's peace—"

She jerked away, her anger spilling over. "I knew it! I knew that was the reason—"

His hand clamped over her mouth solidly. "From there, it evolved into a game, a male ego game. I wanted to see if I could still attract a woman without her knowing who I really was—my success seems to be a bigger draw at times than I am, and I didn't want it to be that way with you and me, Harri—"

Pushing his hand aside, she glared at him. "You actually thought your success would make a difference to me? You *seriously* thought I was that shallow?"

"I don't know what I thought, but obviously I was wrong."

"You didn't have to lie to me."

"No, I didn't, and I've paid for that mistake dearly."

"Why wouldn't you want the world to know who you are?"

"Because, a writer—particularly one whose has made it big in the publishing world and who values his privacy—can take a pseudonym. Not that he doesn't want and appreciate the public's approval. I value my readers, they can make or break me. But I'm also an average guy, a guy who enjoys going to the grocery store for a loaf of bread, or going to a movie, or eating out without being noticed. Writing is a profession, a job, and there are times when an author needs to forget his work. That's not always possible when he becomes a celebrity.

"I don't know why I misled you the day you came after Florence. All I know was that all of a sudden I thought I was confronted again with that damned Harriet Whitlock, the girl with pig tails and horn-rimmed glasses, the girl responsible for making my life a living hell in junior high. That's all I could think of.

"I panicked. Blame it on an inflated ego, stupidity, or call it anything you want. I deserve whatever you think necessary to bring me to my knees, but for God's sake don't throw away what we have, Harri. I love you. You've put me through enough hell to last me a lifetime. I've even tried to write down what I feel for you so I could send it through the mail, hoping you'd have to read it, but I can't find the words—can you imagine? I make my living with words, but I can't find anything that even comes remotely close to telling you how sorry I am or how much I love you. Listen to me—I didn't count on falling in love with you, Harriet, but I did—deeply in love, and then I didn't know how to repair what I'd done. I'd give everything I own to go back and start over, but that's impossible.

"I've watched the way you poured your heart into the book, and don't think I didn't feel guilty for letting you think I was still a struggling writer, but I didn't want to hurt you. But by then, the ruse had gone too far." He drew her to him tightly, trying to erase the tears running down her cheeks. "I made a terrible mistake: I lied to you. I don't make a practice of lying, but in this case, I did, and I'm paying the price. I'm sorry—God, I'm sorry. I wouldn't hurt you for the world."

The music died away, and they stood on the dance floor, holding each other, looking into each other's eyes.

"I'm sorry. My emotions are worn to the bone—there's nothing more I can do or say or give to you," he said softly. "It's up to you, now."

Gazing at him, she realized that her nose was running and her mascara was streaking. "Shae—I don't know what to say—I'm hurt right now, really hurt," she confessed broken-heartedly.

"Will you at least think about what I've just said?"

Squeezing his hand mutely, she nodded.

"That's all I ask."

Reaching into his pocket, he drew out the folded check for one hundred thousand dollars and pressed it into her hand. Turning, he started away as the last strains of the violin faded.

Harri watched him go, feeling more confused than she had ever felt in her whole life.

She longed to believe that he hadn't meant to hurt her, but could she dare hand him her heart again? She had done it so often in the past, only to have him hand it back to her bruised and tattered.

She wasn't sure she could risk that again—even for Shae Malone.

The book was finished.

Shae had sent a brief note through the mail, thanking Harri for her contributions and informing her of the publishing date.

Another week passed. Harri had more flowers sitting in her living room than the maternity ward of Cloverdale hospital, but there seemed to be no solution to the impasse. She wasn't sure what she was waiting for; she just knew she was the most miserable soul on earth.

Deciding to go for a bike ride late Saturday, Harri changed into shorts and placed Magnolia on the handle bars.

As she pedaled down her drive she glanced to see if Shae was home. Disappointed, she saw that his Corvette wasn't in the drive.

Each day was an exercise in futility for her. No

matter what he'd done, she still loved him. He had lied to her, yes, but at least he had been big enough to admit his mistake, and humbly asked to be forgiven.

She wished she could say she was perfect and had never deceived another soul, but she couldn't even come close to claiming that. So what was she waiting for? Why didn't she go to him?

It wasn't the lie that bothered her. In her heart, she just couldn't believe that he had actually fallen in love with her. She was afraid to believe, afraid to take the chance of being hurt again.

Shae Malone in love with Harriet Whitlock? It even sounded ludicrous to her, and yet she wanted to believe it so badly.

Pedaling down the street, it suddenly occurred to her that she had never really thought of Shae being Perry Beal.

Strange, she idolized Perry Beal's writing, yet it was the thought of Shae Malone that sent funny little shivers rippling through her stomach.

A car came careening around the corner, forcing Harri to swerve to the side. As she muttered under her breath, her bicycle went sailing over the curb, pitching monkey and rider head first over the handle bars.

Brakes squealed, and a car door slammed as Harri tried to sit up. With a sigh of disgust, she surveyed the layer of mud on her white shorts. Her knee was torn and bleeding in two different places.

She glanced up to look at the idiot driver who'd done this to her when she saw Shae running toward her. His face had turned the color of his gray three-piece business suit.

Kneeling down beside her, he began to examine her injuries, his eyes skimming her anxiously. "Oh, damn, Harri—I didn't see you, sweetheart—are you hurt?"

Magnolia hopped off the wreckage, and scurried up Shae's shoulder, chattering excitedly.

"No, I'm all right—but Shae, you're going to kill someone if you don't slow down," Harri blurted irritably.

"I know—I know—my mind was a million miles away," he apologized. Setting Magnolia back on the ground, he ran his hands up and down Harri's small frame to feel for broken bones. "Where does it hurt?"

"I'm all right," she insisted. "I think I've just turned my ankle."

Lifting her to her feet, Shae watched as she applied weight to her left foot and winced. "It's sprained."

Scooping her up in his arms, he carried her to his car, whistling for Magnolia to follow.

"Where are you taking me?"

"To the hospital."

"No, Shae, please!" She hated having doctors poking around her!

Loading Harri into the passenger seat, Shae gently set the monkey on her lap. As he slipped behind the wheel, he glanced back at her. "Pipe down, I'm taking you to the emergency room."

"Shae, that's not necessary," she protested again. "I'm fine except for my ankle."

"You're going anyway," he said in a voice that brooked no argument.

An hour later, she had been checked and released from the hospital. Shae had paced the waiting room floor like a caged animal, terrified that the doctor would find a more serious injury.

When they arrived back at her house, he carried her upstairs to her bedroom and deposited her on her bed.

"The animals need to be fed," she murmured, beginning to feel slightly drowsy from the light sedative the doctor had given her.

"Don't worry about a thing. I'll take care of everything."

He left the room and she dozed, faintly hearing him rattle around downstairs with the cages.

"I'll have my orange, please!"

"You'll get an apple and like it," she heard him return calmly.

A moment later, she heard Myron rummaging around in the bottom of his cage, sounding peeved.

Grinning, she drifted off to sleep in a world that suddenly seemed right again.

Eleven

The smell of meatloaf brought Harri awake an hour later. It was dark in her bedroom now. The sound of cicadas tuning up for the night drifted through the window.

Opening her eyes slowly, she shifted lethargically. She could hear Shae moving about below in the kitchen, preparing dinner. Oddly enough, she felt drained of anger and at peace with him for the first time in a long time. Her eyes drifted closed again, savoring the feeling of contentment as she listened to him talking to Myron as he worked.

She was in love with him. Her pain had eased, and she realized that her life was meaningless without him.

A man who was able to admit his mistake, make his own jelly, share the sofa with a lion cub, tolerate a monkey on his back, hold his own in an argument with a mynah bird, plus allow a very stubborn woman the time she desperately needed to overcome her disappointment—without losing his patience—surely couldn't be all that bad.

"Hi, sleepyhead."

Harri opened her eyes to find that special man standing in the doorway, smiling at her. "Hungry?"

Rolling to her side lazily, she smiled back at him. "Uh-huh," she said, nodding. "Something smells delicious."

"It is delicious. I make the best meatloaf on four continents."

Sliding to the middle of the bed, she made a place for him on the bed beside her.

"I've even got a pan of homemade biscuits in the oven," he bragged.

"Oh, yeah? The bang 'em on the counter and dig 'em out of the can kind of homemade?"

"Yeah." Leaning over, he dropped a kiss on her lips, soft as a whisper, and said, "To go with my strawberry jam."

"Then I hope you've brought another jar. I've scraped the other one clean," she confessed.

His hand eased over her hip and lingered. "I thought you were getting a little hippy."

"I am not!"

"You are too!" He leaned down to steal another long kiss.

Catching his hair in her fingers, she drew him close to her breast and held him. He felt so good, so right. "Shae, lie down with me," she whispered.

He didn't answer for a moment, then murmured, "No, if I do," pressing his lips to her throat, "my biscuits will burn."

Their mouths drifted back together and held for a very long time. Shae felt a rush of heady desire, but made himself go slowly. This time he wasn't going to allow her the opportunity to walk away from him so easily.

When their lips parted, they gazed at each other. "I'm glad you're home," she confessed.

"I am too." Reaching for his jacket, he removed a piece of paper and handed it to her.

"What's this?"

"The dedication for the new book." He reached over to switch on the lamp beside the bed. "Read it, then I have to go back to the kitchen and mash my potatoes."

"Honestly, Shae . . . mash your potatoes," Harri grumbled. He could be so unromantic at times. She unfolded the paper and read the inscription: "To Harriet Whitlock—My Beloved Curse. Sorry it took me fifteen years, Harri, but I love you. Please marry me, and let me spend the rest of my life proving it."

Lifting her eyes to his, her gaze softened. "Shae, you realize you've just incriminated yourself before millions of readers."

"Read the copyright."

"Shae, no . . ." She knew before she read it what he had done. The copyright read: Shae Malone and Harriet Whitlock.

His hand came up to cover her mouth gently. "Harri, yes. It's our book. . . . I wouldn't have it any other way. It's something we've created together."

"But I never meant it to be that way. I was only trying to help you . . . Her gaze dropped sheepishly. She still felt absurd when she thought about her efforts to instruct Perry Beal on how to write a mystery.

"And you did help me. Lila, my editor, said it's the best damn job of plotting she's ever read."

Her eyes filled with pride. "Really?"

"Really."

"What's the title?"

"I don't know. I've left that up to you. Now," he slapped his hands on his knees, dismissing the subject, "do you like carrots or peas with meatloaf?"

"Carrots."

"You got it." Rising, he went back to the kitchen to mash his potatoes.

Harri stayed in bed two days with her ankle. The doctor had recommended she stay there at least three, but by late Tuesday afternoon, she was able to move about more comfortably.

Shae had refused to leave her side, except at night. Each evening, he tucked her into bed, gave her a brief good-night kiss, then left her alone while he went to sleep in her parents' bedroom.

Not that she preferred it that way, but he gave no indication he wanted it any differently.

By day, he cared for the animals, and cleaned her house like a domestic goddess. Harri could see her reflection in the kitchen floor, and her mother's solid oak end tables had never looked better.

But having him so close, yet so far away, was the hardest thing for her to tolerate. She lay in her bed at night listening to him move about, aching to be with him, longing to feel him lying next to her.

Other than stealing an occasional, friendly kiss, he left her alone.

She tried to tell herself that he was giving her

time, but it was time that she no longer wanted. Yet how could she tell him that without appearing to chase him again?

By the end of the week there was no longer any excuse for him to hang around. Shae came down the stairway carrying his duffel bag right after dinner Wednesday evening to find Harri sprawled on the sofa reading the funny papers. He had given her a week, but she had yet to respond to his marriage proposal.

"Your mom called while you were in the shower," he said.

"Yes, I talked to her a minute ago. They're on their way home . . ." Glancing up, she spotted the bag in his hand and frowned. "Are you going somewhere?"

He shrugged. "I thought it was time I got out of your way."

Lowering the paper, she said softly, "You're not in my way."

She hated the thought of his leaving. Even more, she hated the thought that he even wanted to.

"I have an appointment with a realtor to put Gram's house up for sale," he said, walking toward the door. "Don't give Myron any more orange tonight. He just spit a piece onto the floor, and I stepped on it and almost broke my neck."

"Shae . . ." Harri sat up straighter, realizing that he was actually going.

Pausing with his hand on the doorknob, he turned back to face her. "Yes?"

"I . . . well, thank you." She wasn't going to beg him to stay. If he wanted to go, he could.

"No sweat. You know where I am if you need me."

"But . . . can't you stay a little longer?" she said lamely, biting back her rising panic.

"I could stay," he shrugged, "but what's the point? You're able to get around okay now, aren't you? You don't need me."

"I'm better," she admitted.

Meeting her pleading gaze, he said softly, "Well, like I said, you know where I am . . . if you need me."

A moment later, she heard the screen door close behind him.

Silence closed in on her. The house echoed like an empty tomb without his presence.

Pulling herself off the sofa, she limped slowly across the room into the kitchen for a drink of water.

"Shae's sorry, Big Mama. Shae *looooves* Big Mama."

Harri glanced at Myron, realizing that Shae hadn't been devoting all his time to dishwashing this past week. He'd put in a few hours bird training.

You know where I am if you need me.

His words haunted her as she left the kitchen and began to climb the long stairway. What was he trying to tell her?

Shae came to me. Perhaps he's waiting for me to show that I love him enough to go to him.

Entering her bedroom, Harri paused.

Was that what he was trying to discover? That she loved him enough to swallow her pride and admit that she had nursed her pride about enough?

Sitting down on the side of her bed, she thought about the past few weeks. They had been the longest, most miserable of her life.

They were both at fault.

They had been apart for years, and in view of the way she had chased him when they were younger, he had good reason to be leery of her in the beginning.

And if she were to be honest, wasn't she still chasing him?

Hadn't she deliberately changed out of her jeans and into that skimpy garter belt and black hose when she'd overheard him telling Mike he needed to borrow coffee? She flushed, recalling the way she had brazenly paraded herself in front of him, knowing he was a red-blooded, all-American male, who'd hardly be able to overlook a half-naked woman, even if she was Harriet the Curse.

Didn't she remove her bra and wear the tightest halter tops and the skimpiest shorts she could find to mow her lawn when, in the past, she'd always worn old sweats and her dad's enormous tee shirts?

Yes, he had deceived her, but his was an honest mistake. Her actions had been more devious. And God love him, he had done everything within his power to correct his mistake.

He even proposed to you, Harriet, in front of twenty million readers. Shae Malone, telling twenty million fans that he was sorry, and that he loved Harriet Whitlock.

And dumb old Harriet hadn't even told him that she'd accept.

Across the lawn, Shae lay in bed, his hands laced behind his head, staring at the ceiling.

He had been like this for thirty minutes, and sleep still eluded him. Listening to the crickets outside his window, he wrestled with his conscience. Had he taken too big a gamble this time? Instead should he just have swept her up into his arms and hauled her into the bedroom to demand that she marry him?

A week had gone by since he had shown her the dedication for his book. Seven long days—and she hadn't even mentioned if she would or wouldn't marry him. She had ignored his proposal, which somehow felt worse than a refusal.

Dammit, Harri. I can't take much more of this!

He felt like a kid begging for candy in the checkout lane.

Well, Malone, at least you can't accuse her of loving you for your bankroll. Your so-called success doesn't mean a gnat's ass to her!

Well, so be it. He'd give her just another few minutes then he—

"Yes."

Startled, Shae glanced toward the darkened doorway. Moonlight streamed through the open window, revealing a figure standing in the shadows.

"Yes, what?"

"Yes, I'll marry you."

"And?" he prompted.

"And . . . I need you . . . I really do."

A grin creased the corners of his mouth. He felt relieved he didn't have to go after her. "Go on, Whitlock, confession is good for the soul."

"And I've been wrong, too, and I'm sorry. I shouldn't have chased you then—and I shouldn't be chasing you now." Her voice grew very small. "But I have loved you from the moment I laid eyes on you fifteen years ago. I can't help myself, Shae, that's just the way it is, and probably always will be."

Lifting the sheet, he invited her to join him. "Come over here and say that again."

As she slipped between the sheets, he caught her scent. Gardenias. He suddenly loved gardenias.

Their mouths met for a long, leisurely exploration.

"Isn't there something else you wanted to say?" he murmured, planting feather kisses on her shoulders, then her neck.

"No."

"You're sure?"

"Shae—do I have to say it?"

"I'd like to hear it—I think you owe me that."

"Oh, okay—I'm sorry about taking your bathing suit," she said, relenting. "It was childish and unreasonable of me to leave you running around naked."

"You bet your sweet tush it was." He ran kisses over her face feeling her breathing quicken. "Now, we're going to get dressed, find a Justice of the Peace, and get this thing settled between us, once and for all. The big church wedding can wait a few weeks."

"No way. You'll get cold feet and walk out on me like you did Kristen."

"Not a chance." Reaching for her hand, he placed it on the proof that he wouldn't.

Taking his hand, she guided it to her middle.

He issued a low groan when he realized what she was wearing. "Oh, hell, not the garter belt again—not the garter belt!"

"Shae, I have to be honest with you." Harri sighed. "I am never going to give this garter belt up."

Settling back on the pillow, she could tell that he didn't mind.

"You do, and I'll have five more in your closet by nightfall."

Grinning, they kissed again.

"Are you mad at me?"

"About what?"

"About my admitting that after all these years, I'm still chasing you?"

Lifting his head, his eyes traveled lazily over her body, drinking in all the dips and curves and fullness. "I hate to disillusion you, my love, but in case you haven't noticed, I haven't been running away for a very long time."

"Oh?" Her brow lifted as he continued to gaze at her in the light of the moon spilling across the bed.

"Yeah, how do you feel about moving to New York?"

"I'd like that."

"Good, can you be ready to leave by Monday?"

She nodded. Mike would understand if she gave short notice, and she'd get in touch with the Bronx zoo. Their eyes met again. "See anything you like, Malone?"

"I see one or two or three things that interest me, Whitlock." His hand reached to lower the top of her chemise. "The garter belt stays on."

"Of course."

Their mouths touched, played. "I'm sorry I've been so impossible," she whispered.

His mouth lowered to place a kiss on each breast. Closing his eyes, Shae savored the taste of her. "I wouldn't have changed a moment of it."

Perhaps she'd doubted his love before, but never again. As he lifted his head again, it was there for all the world to see, openly shining through his eyes, in his voice.

"You know what, Whitlock?"

"No, what, Malone?"

"I was going to give you another thirty minutes, then I was coming after you," he confessed.

"Really?"

"Really," he whispered, his breath warm against her ear. "You're one hell of a woman, Harriet. I don't know why it's taken me fifteen years to realize that, but I plan to spend the rest of my life making it up to you."

Harri steadied his face with her hands. "I don't want to be Harriet anymore—I want to be just plain Harri."

He shook his head negatively, then dipped down and placed another lingering kiss on each of her breasts.

Mindless, her bones turning to water, Harri murmured, "Why not?"

Lifting his head, he brushed his lips across her mouth. "In another couple of hours, you'll be Harri Malone. I think we'll both like that better."

"Oh—really? In two short hours?"

Easing her even lower, he grinned. "Well, it could take longer. . . ."

But Harriet didn't care. Shae Malone could take all the time he wanted.

THE EDITOR'S CORNER

As is the case with many of you, LOVESWEPT books have been a part of my life for a very long time—since before we ever published book #1, in fact. Having worked with Carolyn Nichols for over seven years, there's no way I could not have been caught up in her enthusiasm for and devotion to the LOVESWEPT project. I hope I can convey my excitement over the wonderful books we publish as entertainingly as Carolyn has over the years in the Editor's Corner.

Since next month is April, we're going to shower you with "keepers." Our six books for the month are sure to coax the sun from behind the clouds and brighten your rainy days.

Continuing her *Once Upon a Time* series, Kay Hooper brings you **WHAT DREAMS MAY COME**, LOVESWEPT #390. Can you imagine what Kelly Russell goes through when, a week before her wedding, her fiancé, John Mitchell, has a tragic accident which leaves him in a coma? Ten years later Kelly is finally putting the past behind her when Mitch arrives on her doorstep, determined to rekindle the love that fate had stolen from them. Kay involves the reader from page one in this poignant, modern-day Rip Van Winkle story. Your emotions will run the gamut as you root for brave survivor Kelly and enigmatic Mitch to bridge the chasm of time and build a new life together.

Sandra Chastain has the remarkable ability to create vivid characters with winning personalities. Her people always lead interesting, purposeful lives—and the hero and heroine in **ADAM'S OUTLAW**, LOVESWEPT #391, are no exceptions. Toni Gresham leads a group of concerned citizens called Peachtree Vigilantes, who are out to corral muggers who prey on the elderly. Instead she swoops down from a tree with a Tarzan yell and lands atop police captain Adam Ware! Adam, who is conducting his own sting operation, is stunned to discover he's being held captive by an angel with golden curls. You'll laugh as the darling renegade tries to teach the lone-wolf lawman a thing or two about helping people—and in return learns a thing or two about love.

I suggest saving Janet Evanovich's **SMITTEN**, LOVESWEPT #392, for one of those rainy days this month. There's no way that after reading this gem of a romance you won't be smiling and floating on air! Single mom Lizabeth Kane wasn't exactly construction worker material, but she

(continued)

figured she could learn. The hours were good—she'd be home by the time her kids were out of school—and the location—the end of her block—was convenient. Matt Hallahan takes one look at her résumé—handwritten on spiral notebook paper—then at the lady herself, and he's instantly smitten. When the virile hunk agrees to hire her, Lizabeth's heart—and her libido—send up a cheer! Lizabeth never knew that painting a wall could be a sensual experience or that the smell of sawdust could be so enticing, but whenever Matt was near, he made her senses sizzle. Janet adds some zany secondary characters to this tender story who are guaranteed to make you laugh. For an uplifting experience, don't miss **SMITTEN!**

April showers occasionally leave behind rainbows. Tami Hoag brings you one rainbow this month and two more over the next several months in the form of her three-book series, *The Rainbow Chasers*. The Fearsome Foursome was what they called themselves, four college friends who bonded together and shared dreams of pursuing their hearts' desires in a sleepy coastal town in northern California. In **HEART OF GOLD**, LOVESWEPT #393, Tami picks up on the lives of the friends as one by one they realize their dreams and find the ends of their personal rainbows. Faith Kincaid is just about to open her inn and begin to forget her former life in Washington, D.C., when elegantly handsome Shane Callan—Dirty Harry in disguise—arrives on assignment to protect her—a government witness in a bribery trial. Faith has never known the intoxicating feeling of having a man want her until Shane pulls her to him on a darkened staircase and makes her yearn for the taste of his lips. Shane, lonely and haunted by demons, realizes Faith is his shot at sanctuary, his anchor in the storm. **HEART OF GOLD** is a richly textured story that you won't be able to put down. But Tami's next in the series won't be far behind! Look for **KEEPING COMPANY** in June and **REILLY'S RETURN** in August. You can spend the entire summer chasing rainbows!

Courtney Henke is one of the brightest new stars on the LOVESWEPT horizon. And for those of you who wrote after reading her first book, **CHAMELEON**, asking for Adam's story, Courtney has granted your wish—and delivered one sensational story in **JINX**, LOVESWEPT #394. How much
(continued)

more romantic can you get than a hero who falls in love with the heroine even before he meets her? It's Diana Machlen's ethereal image in an advertisement for the perfume her family developed that haunts Adam's dreams. But the lady in the flesh is just as tempting, when Adam—on a mission to retrieve from her the only written copy of the perfume formula—encounters the lovely Diana at her cabin in the Missouri Ozarks. Diana greets Adam less than enthusiastically. You see, strange things happen when she gets close to a man—and there's no way she can stay away from Adam! The chain of events is just too funny for words as Adam vows to prove her wrong about her jinx. Don't miss this delightful romp!

Deborah Smith's name has been popping up in more and more of your letters as one of the favorite LOVESWEPT authors. It's no wonder! Deborah has an imagination and creative ability that knows no bounds. In **LEGENDS,** LOVE-SWEPT #395, Deborah wisks you from a penthouse in Manhattan to a tiny village in Scotland. At a lavish party billionaire Douglas Kincaid can't help but follow the mysterious woman in emerald silk onto his terrace. Elgiva MacRoth wants the brutally handsome dealmaker—but only to kidnap him! She holds him captive in order to preserve her heritage and convince him to give up his land holdings in Scotland. But soon it's not clear who is the prisoner and who is the jailer as Douglas melts her resistance and revels in her sensuality. These two characters are so alive, they almost walk right off the pages. Deborah will have you believing in legends before you finish this mesmerizing story.

Look for our sparkling violet covers next month, and enjoy a month of great reading with LOVESWEPT!

Sincerely,

Susann Brailey

Susann Brailey
Editor
LOVESWEPT
Bantam Books
666 Fifth Avenue
New York, NY 10103

FAN OF THE MONTH

Kay Bendall

What a thrill and an honor to be selected a LOVE-SWEPT Fan of the Month! Reading is one of the joys of my life. Through books I enter worlds of enchantment, wonder, adventure, suspense, beauty, fantasy, humor, and, above all else, a place where love conquers all.

My favorite books are LOVESWEPTs. Each and every month I am impressed and delighted with the variety and excellence of the selections. I laugh, cry, am inspired, touched, and enjoy them all.

Kay Hooper, Joan Elliott Pickart, Iris Johansen, Deborah Smith, Barbara Boswell, and Peggy Webb are some of my favorite LOVESWEPT authors. The blend of familiar and new authors ensure that LOVESWEPTs will remain innovative and number one among the romance books.

The day the mailman brings my LOVESWEPTs is my favorite day of the month!

OFFICIAL RULES TO
LOVESWEPT'S
DREAM MAKER GIVEAWAY
(See entry card in center of this book)

1. NO PURCHASE NECESSARY. To enter both the
   sweepstakes and accept the risk-free trial offer, follow the
   directions published on the insert card in this book. Return
   your entry on the reply card provided. If you do not wish to
   take advantage of the risk-free trial offer, but wish to enter the
   sweepstakes, return the entry card only with the "FREE
   ENTRY" sticker attached, or send your name and address on
   a 3x5 card to : Loveswept Sweepstakes, Bantam Books,
   PO Box 985, Hicksville, NY 11802-9827.
2. To be eligible for the prizes offered, your entry must be
   received by September 17, 1990. We are not responsible for
   late, lost or misdirected mail. Winners will be selected on or
   about October 16, 1990 in a random drawing under the
   supervision of Marden Kane, Inc., an independent judging
   organization, and except for those prizes which will be
   awarded to the first 50 entrants, prizes will be awarded after
   that date. By entering this sweepstakes, each entrant accepts
   and agrees to be bound by these rules and the decision of the
   judges which shall be final and binding. This sweepstakes will
   be presented in conjunction with various book offers
   sponsored by Bantam Books under the following titles: Agatha
   Christie "Mystery Showcase", Louis L'Amour "Great American
   Getaway", Loveswept "Dreams Can Come True" and
   Loveswept "Dream Makers". Although the prize options and
   graphics of this Bantam Books sweepstakes will vary in each
   of these book offers, the value of each prize level will be
   approximately the same and prize winners will have the options
   of selecting any prize offered within the prize level won.
3. Prizes in the Loveswept "Dream Maker" sweepstakes: Grand
   Prize (1) 14 Day trip to either Hawaii, Europe or the Caribbean.
   Trip includes round trip air transportation from any major airport
   in the US and hotel accomodations (approximate retail value
   $6,000); Bonus Prize (1) $1,000 cash in addition to the trip;
   Second Prize (1) 27" Color TV (approximate retail value $900).

4. This sweepstakes is open to residents of the US, and Canada (excluding the province of Quebec), who are 18 years of age or older. Employees of Bantam Books, Bantam Doubleday Dell Publishing Group Inc., their affiliates and subsidiaries, Marden Kane Inc. and all other agencies and persons connected with conducting this sweepstakes and their immediate family members are not eligible to enter this sweepstakes. This offer is subject to all applicable laws and regulations and is void in the province of Quebec and wherever prohibited or restricted by law. In order to win a prize, residents of Canada will be required to correctly answer a time-limited arithmetical skill-testing question.

5. Winners will be notified by mail and will be required to execute an affidavit of eligibility and release which must be returned within 14 days of notification or an alternate winner will be selected. Prizes are not transferable. Trip prize must be taken within one year of notification and is subject to airline departure schedules and ticket and accommodation availability. Winner must have a valid passport. No substitution will be made for any prize except as offered. If a prize should be unavailable at sweepstakes end, sponsor reserves the right to substitute a prize of equal or greater value. Winners agree that the sponsor, its affiliates, and their agencies and employees shall not be liable for injury, loss or damage of any kind resulting from an entrant's participation in this offer or from the acceptance or use of the prizes awarded. Odds of winning are dependant upon the number of entries received. Taxes, if any, are the sole responsibility of the winners. Winner's entry and acceptance of any prize offered constitutes permission to use the winner's name, photograph or other likeness for purposes of advertising and promotion on behalf of Bantam Books and Bantam Doubleday Dell Publishing Group Inc. without additional compensation to the winner.

6. For a list of winners (available after 10/16/90), send a self addressed stamped envelope to Bantam Books Winners List, PO Box 704, Sayreville, NJ 08871.

7. The free gifts are available only to entrants who also agree to sample the Loveswept subscription program on the terms described. The sweepstakes prizes offered by affixing the "Free Entry" sticker to the Entry Form are available to all entrants, whether or not an entrant chooses to affix the "Free Books" sticker to the Entry Form.

60 Minutes to a Better, More Beautiful You!

Now it's easier than ever to awaken your sensuality, stay slim forever—even make yourself irresistible. With Bantam's bestselling subliminal audio tapes, you're only 60 minutes away from a better, more beautiful you!

__ 45004-2	**Slim Forever**	$8.95
__ 45112-X	**Awaken Your Sensuality**	$7.95
__ 45081-6	**You're Irresistible**	$7.95
__ 45035-2	**Stop Smoking Forever**	$8.95
__ 45130-8	**Develop Your Intuition**	$7.95
__ 45022-0	**Positively Change Your Life**	$8.95
__ 45154-5	**Get What You Want**	$7.95
__ 45041-7	**Stress Free Forever**	$7.95
__ 45106-5	**Get a Good Night's Sleep**	$7.95
__ 45094-8	**Improve Your Concentration**	$7.95
__ 45172-3	**Develop A Perfect Memory**	$8.95

THE DELANEY DYNASTY

Men and women whose loves an passions are so glorious
it takes many great romance novels by three bestselling
authors to tell their tempestuous stories.

THE SHAMROCK TRINITY

☐	21975	**RAFE, THE MAVERICK** *by Kay Hooper*	$2.95
☐	21976	**YORK, THE RENEGADE** *by Iris Johansen*	$2.95
☐	21977	**BURKE, THE KINGPIN** *by Fayrene Preston*	$2.95

THE DELANEYS OF KILLAROO

☐	21872	**ADELAIDE, THE ENCHANTRESS** *by Kay Hooper*	$2.75
☐	21873	**MATILDA, THE ADVENTURESS** *by Iris Johansen*	$2.75
☐	21874	**SYDNEY, THE TEMPTRESS** *by Fayrene Preston*	$2.75

THE DELANEYS: *The Untamed Years*

☐	21899	**GOLDEN FLAMES** *by Kay Hooper*	$3.50
☐	21898	**WILD SILVER** *by Iris Johansen*	$3.50
☐	21897	**COPPER FIRE** *by Fayrene Preston*	$3.50

Buy them at your local bookstore or use this page to order.

Bantam Books, Dept. SW7, 414 East Golf Road, Des Plaines, IL 60016

Please send me the items I have checked above. I am enclosing $_____
(please add $2.00 to cover postage and handling). Send check or money
order, no cash or C.O.D.s please.

Mr/Ms _____

Address _____

City/State _____ Zip_____

Please allow four to six weeks for delivery.
Prices and availability subject to change without notice.